Going
❀
Down
❀
Slow

Going Down Slow

John Metcalf

McClelland and Stewart Limited/Toronto

The Canadian Publishers
McClelland and Stewart Limited
25 Hollinger Road, Toronto 374

Grateful acknowledgement is made to the publisher
for permission to reprint material from Compton
Mackenzie, *The Passionate Elopement*, 1911,
Macdonald & Co. (Publishers) Ltd.

Every effort has been made to trace ownership of
copyright material. Information will be welcome
that will enable the publisher to rectify any
omission.

Printed and bound in Canada by
The Hunter Rose Company

This book is for

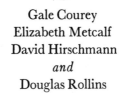

Gale Courey
Elizabeth Metcalf
David Hirschmann
and
Douglas Rollins

The men don't know what the little girls understand.
Howling Wolf

Chapter One

The window had ice on the inside again. Even the folded issues of the Montreal *Gazette* which were stuffed into the gaps of the window-frame were glazed. They looked like the long ribbly icicles of a frozen waterfall. David watched the faint trails of his breath. Or stalactites.

"With one bound," he said, "David leaped from the bed and rushed, laughing, under the cold shower."

Nothing.

The window looked out onto a square ventilation shaft in the middle of the building, as did windows of the other three apartments on the third floor. What the shaft was supposed to be ventilating he'd never been able to work out. The fourth floor was the top floor and from his bed David could see the glooming sky. Swaddling the army blankets about him, he sat up in bed and pulled the shade down so that he wouldn't run the risk of seeing the Scots lady again without her clothes on.

(He'd stopped pulling down the shade at night because it had shot up on several occasions by its own volition jacking him from sleep with a carbine-CRACK. He had been left staring rigid in the dark, listening to the animal scuffling noises as the blind lapped round and round its roller – all the essential functions of his body diminished.)

He heard Jim slam into the bathroom and the nest of wire coat-hangers on the back of the door jangled and tapped, jangled.

Twenty-five past seven by his *Jock* alarm-clock.

A strange name for a clock.

"As David and his chums neared the camp," he said, "the air was filled with the aroma of frying bacon."

Wind shook the window-pane. Beyond the yellowing blind, the sky was full and grey with snow. David decided that he was probably ill. His head ached. His throat. His throat was definitely dry and sore. Doubtless infected. He pictured the inside of his throat as being like the neck of a guitar strung with red tendons. And now the tendons were studded with white and yellow lumps of infection. Lumps? *Nodules*. Studded with nodules of infection.

He got out of bed, switched on the light, and walked across the freezing, gritty linoleum to look in the mirror ($1.25 in *Woodhouse's Annual Sale*. Small defect. i.e. broken). He was definitely pale. Any sensible man would have stayed in bed.

Susan's black silk scarf lay crumpled on the chest of drawers beside the mirror. He ran its smoothness over his palm, touched its softness to his face. She had left it there on Thursday. The warmth of his face raised the ghost of her perfume.

"Nice. *Italian Straw Hat*."

"You always say that."

"*Straw Hat*, then. Still nice."

"Why do you always say 'Italian'?"

Mumbling into her hair.

"I don't know ... I think it was a film ..."

Jim was sitting in the dining room eating *Rice Krispies* and reading the back of the box. A sheepskin coat was draped over his shoulders. David went into the kitchen and opened the fridge. It contained a gallon jug of *Queberac* and a sock.

"Any milk?"

"Yes, there is. No thanks to you."

David took a bowl from the heap of dishes in the big double sink and holding it under the hot tap started to scrape at it with a knife. Old *Rice Krispies* solid as rivets.

"It's been your turn for three days now," called Jim.

"I'll do them tonight."

"Good job – because buggered if *I* will."

"Did you use all the coffee?"

"Yes. And you know why, don't you."

"Oh, for Christ's sake! I'll do the *dishes* tonight and I'll do the *shopping* tonight. O.K.?"

"Don't let me inconvenience you in any way," said Jim.

"Bollocks," said David.

He gave up trying to clean the bowl and searched through the cupboard for an old packet of Chinese tea. On one side of the packet was a simpering creature in a purple robe holding a yellow parasol. Underneath the picture were the words:

This tea purifies the blood and is very hernthy.

He stuck his head through the serving-hatch into the dining room and said, "Hey, Jim."

"What?"

"I think I've got inflamed nodules."

Jim shrugged the coat higher on his shoulders.

"You shouldn't screw so much," he said.

David poured boiling water over the tea-leaves in the mug and then stood with the kettle in his hand staring at the grease-sputtered wall behind the stove.

"Jim?"

He went over to the serving-hatch again.

"Jim? Do you think she *really* phoned the school?"

"Oh, Holy Fuck! Not *again*! I *don't know* if she phoned. I *don't know* what'll happen. I *don't know* if it's serious. You're going to find out, aren't you? This morning."

"Yes," said David.

The rusting scabby radiator beside the lavatory was the warmest in the apartment. Sitting on the lavatory, David sipped the tea. His mind started to circle the question. During the weekend he had rehearsed the evidence into worn patterns, repeated sentences until they had become the incantations of his anxiety, flat formulae, nothingnesses.

Susan's mother said she had phoned the school on Friday.

She had told Susan this on Friday evening.

She said she had evidence that one of the teachers had seduced Susan.

She knew the teacher was young and had not been long at the school.

She claimed to have spoken to Vice-Principal McPhee.

McPhee had promised an immediate investigation.

BUT

Susan denied everything.

Susan's mother was unbalanced and gave that impression in conversation. Her evidence would. ' . be suspect.

She had claimed to have phoned authorities before. Last year, the RCMP.

McPhee had attended a meeting of the Board on Friday and had been absent from school all day.

Susan thought it probable her mother hadn't phoned at all.

David stared at his white drip-dry shirt which was hanging from the string over the bath. Even though he'd spent ten minutes with his toothbrush on the collar and cuffs, the shirt still looked yellowish and grubby. How could he say, "I will continue this conversation only in the presence of my lawyer," when his shirt was grubby? It was all very well for Jim with his dyspeptic-aristocrat face. Jim could doubtless say something bored and weary – "Rather dodgy to prove, McPhee, unless one had been caught *in flagrante delicto*. Which I don't recall."

But *he* wasn't Jim. And as he didn't *have* a lawyer, what could he do in McPhee's office under McPhee's steel eyes? Scuffle through the *Yellow Pages*?

God rot the bloody woman! Even if she hadn't phoned, she'd got hold of *something*. What could her "evidence" be? An overheard phone-conversation? Being seen together? But that wouldn't have told her his age and how long he'd been at the school. Who would have told her only that much? Why not his name?

It didn't make sense. It just didn't fit together. Still, with Susan denying any relationship, he was saved from the worst possibilities. If she was young enough anyway. Whatever the Quebec age was. Saved from the possibility of statutory rape charges.

On Friday night when she'd phoned to warn him, she'd been crying. She'd called at about twelve-thirty, whispering on the extension-phone in her bedroom. Her mother was working herself into permanent hysteria; she had flushed Susan's goldfish down the lavatory, shouting,

See what happens to the goldfishes of whores!

Her father had been raging and had hit her in the face. The whisper had been cut mid-sentence. He had been left listening to the dial-tone.

He wished he could have seen her, spoken to her over the weekend. . . .

He didn't know how she survived in that madhouse where conversations were bellowed competitions with the TV, where her father ate raw meat and her mother believed in the Evil Eye.

Her mother had come to Canada from Lebanon at the age of nine. She had been put to work immediately by a cousin who owned a dry-goods store near Saskatoon. She'd learned to speak and write English as best she could. At home she spoke Arabic. Most of her day was spent in shopping for food at the Jean Talon market and in cooking the many dishes that made up the evening meal – homus bi tahini, ba ba ghannouj, kibbee and snobar, kafta, shishlik, laban with cucumber, harisse, mahalabia. Her knowledge of the world outside her home was sketchy and confined to what she understood of television, *Ladies' Home Journal* and *Modern Screen*.

Last year, she had decided that Susan "reeked of LSD" and claimed to have phoned the RCMP who had gladly agreed to follow Susan everywhere she went.

She often cut photographs of suave and handsome men from *Ladies' Home Journal* and left them about Susan's room. On the photos she wrote, "The man Susan will marry."

She habitually wrote on the covers of Susan's paperbacks; under the photos of authors she wrote "Nasty" or "Ugly" or "A criminal."

She often put scraps of blue cloth into Susan's purse to ward off the Evil Eye.

Whenever Susan disobeyed her by coming home late, she found spread out on her bed receipts going back five years from doctors,

15

dentists, and drug-stores. A note in red pencil would say, "Total now $1117.53." In the fridge, notes saying, "None of this good food for Susan."

She had told him less about her father. All he really knew was that her father owned a clothing store in the east end; that he was six feet two, immensely strong, a dark man, and given to insane rages.

When Susan's mother had told him the news, he had stamped on one of Susan's Coltrane records, called her a whore, slapped her face, torn in half her *Penguin* edition of *The Brothers Karamazov* and smashed her Buddha with a hammer.

When he had calmed down, he had paced the apartment from room to room shouting curses –

May his bowels pass rocks!
May ill-fortune befall the camel that favoured his mother!
A disease like leprosy should eat his face!
etc.

He had kept shouting "With these hands!" holding them up like a surgeon for the rubber gloves.

"With these hands.

I'm going to kill him.

With my own hands.

He's going to die.

With my own two hands. . . ."

David peered into the mirror at his foaming teeth. His toothbrush tasted of *Tide*. He found himself wondering about those hands, wondering if they were hairy, if they had torn *The Brothers Karamazov* lengthways or crossways.

If she *had* phoned, if McPhee had returned to school after three-thirty on Friday, there were about nine possible suspects. Or she could have phoned McPhee at his home. Nine possibles. Five nondescripts who taught grades eight and nine – even McPhee wouldn't consider them for long – and then four who taught senior grades. Bill Jock-strap, Henry Stamp-Club, Visual Aid and himself.

(Tell Susan to be seen, to be seen frequently, talking to Henry Stamp-Club. Still waters run deep.)

With a low belch, a wodge of tea-leaves and bits from the kitchen sink came up in the bath-tub. David stared at the mess in sudden fury.

"OH, SHIT!"

He might be coming home without a job and even with legal trouble on his hands; there was the possibility of being savaged by a mad Arab; the bloody dishes had to be bloody washed; he had to do the bloody shopping; and *now*, because it was also his turn to deal with him, he'd have to lie in wait for Monsieur idle sodding Gagnon and force him to drag his idle sodding three hundred pound paunch up the stairs and then BRIBE the smelly bugger with a large *Molson* while he gazed at the pipes and U-trap:

sacrament!

overwhelmed by the immensity of the job

tabernac!

his belt-buckle where most people keep their genitals

sighs

wipes nose on biceps

That fucker, my friend –

gestures at U-trap with slimy, reeking *Old Port* butt

– she's solid fucking rust

subsides –

krisse-la

      – onto one knee like circus elephant

operates wrench

'STIE!

wrench

Yes, sir! You know what you 'ave there?

No.

Eh? Right in there. You know what you 'ave?

No.

You 'ave yourself a blockage.

"OH, SHIT!" shouted David.

Hours of it. Bloody *hours* of it. Hours of unfunny vaudeville.

"SHIT, SHIT, SHIT!" yelled David and hurled the bar of soap into the tub.

Jim banged on the door.

"Christ, you're not even dressed yet," he said. "I want to be out of here by eight. O.K.?"

"Nearly ready," said David, buttoning his shirt. The collar felt clammy.

"And this afternoon," said Jim. "I'm not hanging about while you talk to kids. Be ready at the side entrance at three-thirty."

"What's the rush?"

"I've got to eat and be at McGill for six. Seen my razor?"

"I thought lectures were Thursdays."

"Ah, well it's a special treat tonight. An intellectual feast that Noddy and Big Ears have arranged."

"What's it about?"

"Fuck knows. Some stimulating twat from Toronto. It's called *Towards a Taxonomy of Educational Criteria*."

"Sounds a fascinating load of old *ca-ca*."

"If not smegma," said Jim.

"I don't know how you stand the boredom of whoring after all that shit."

Jim shrugged and carried on cleaning out his razor with the little brush.

"Just keep Education's First Law in mind, Jim. Shit Floats."

"Charming."

"Well . . . fuck it," said David. "Have fun."

"Have fun teaching high school for the rest of your life."

David turned away as Jim snapped the razor shut and flushed the lavatory. Then he stuck his head round the door again and said, "Hey, Jim. I've just thought of a joke. If Noddy asked you what you thought of this Taxonomy thing, you could tell him that as far as you were concerned he could stuff it."

Jim looked at his watch. "We're leaving in exactly seven minutes," he said. He plugged the razor in.

David went into the living room and started to gather up the exercise-books which were scattered on the floor around his arm-chair. He stood in front of the window counting them. Thirty. Two missing.

He stood looking out across the snow-blown roofs to the huge sign above Ste. Catherine Street. Bright bands of running colour – red, green, yellow, red again and then

Canada Tire
Canada Tire
Canada Tire

The garish colours and alien spelling had irritated him for more than a year now. Five more months. The lease would be up in June. Five months too before the sun appeared again.

Two missing.

The light fixtures were gothic candles dripping with plastic wax and surmounted by strawberry bakelite shades.

When they had landed in Montreal they had spent their first three days in the "Y". Depressed by Gideon Bibles and naked admirers in the washrooms, they'd quickly signed a two-year lease. After student rooms in England, the apartment had seemed palatial. It was not for some time that they discovered that most apartments were cheaper, cleaner, better furnished, had double windows, were warm inside, and disposed of garbage more efficiently and regularly than was Monsieur Gagnon's custom.

Every night the sign washed the black, uncurtained window red, green, yellow, red again and then

Canada Tire
Canada Tire
Canada Tire

It served him as a focus for all his feelings of dispossession, prejudice and xenophobia. He brooded about the sign. He had fantasies of blowing it up, fusing it, of taking evening courses at Sir George Williams University in Electrical Engineering and Neon Tubery.

One evening the sign would start to hum; the hum would rise to a whine, to an agony of sound. The gawking crowds along Ste. Catherine Street would press their hands over their ears. The bands of colour would race faster, glow brighter, until an apocalypse of light would spell

CANADA TYRE
and die.

"Ready?" yelled Jim.

"One minute!"

Two books missing. Given the kind of day this was likely to be, the books were bound to belong to Gertrude Nemeroff

(green teeth, fetid perspiration, mother also a teacher for the Board and therefore dangerous)

and Alan Johnson

(hideous with terminal acne, persistent)

What about my MARK? How are you going to give me a MARK if you've lost . . .

"For Christ's *sake*!" called Jim.

David zipped up the heavy jacket and wedged the pile of exercise-books under his arm.

"Sorry," he said.

Jim opened the door. Two *Dominion* bags full of garbage toppled in on his legs and feet.

"Oh, Jesus Christ!" said David.

Tea-leaves, melon-rind, brown slimy lettuce, spaghetti, a Heinz baked beans can.

"Hey!" said David. "He must have done that on purpose. We left them against the wall."

Jim did not say anything.

A squashed container from the *Nanking* oozed cold plum sauce.

"The dirty sod!" said David stepping out over the mess. "What's he think he's playing at?"

Jim waggled his foot, shaking off the tea-leaves. He inserted the ferrule of his umbrella and clattered the bean can across the small landing. He speared up the melon-rind and dropped it down the stairwell.

"This is *it*," he said.

"It's like the bloody middle ages," said David.

They boomed down the lino-covered stairs into the lobby. Jim stopped in front of Gagnon's apartment and rapped on the *Superintendent* sign.

There was no answer.

"Gagnon! This is Wilson from 302!"

The usual stench hung about the apartment – cooking, cat-piss, stale sweat, children, shit.

"Smells as if he's got a bucket of carrion simmering away on the stove," said David.

"Gagnon!" shouted Jim. "Come out!"

They listened.

Inside the apartment something fell to the floor.

"Perhaps he's drunk again," said David.

"At eight-fifteen?" said Jim.

He smashed on the door with his umbrella handle leaving three dents in the brown paint.

"Maudit anglais!" shouted Gagnon from within.

"I'll be back at four, Gagnon!" shouted Jim.

A woman's voice screamed something.

"You'd better have that shit cleaned up by the time I get back! By four o'clock!"

"Mange d'la merde, maudit krisse!" shouted Gagnon.

"Four o'clock!" shouted Jim.

They listened.

As they walked away across the loud tiles, they heard the lock and chain on Gagnon's door. He did not look out but shouted. "And you, my friend, can lick my ass!"

"Va te faire enculer par les Grecs!" shouted Jim.

The lobby door swung to behind them and they were out in the cutting wind.

"We're going to have to fix him," said David. "Speak to the rental office woman or something."

"What can one expect of a people," said Jim, "who pronounce Ulysses – 'Youlease'?"

The wheels of Jim's *Volkswagen* were frozen fast. He set to work kicking them free while David chipped the ice off the windshield. Particles of ice flew into his cuff and up his sleeve. The wind drilled into his forehead, made his head ache.

While the engine coughed and tried to turn, David sat motionless in the frozen car. The hairs in his nose were frozen. His hands were white, aching from holding the icy scraper. Piles were inevitable. Two more winters of sitting in frozen cars on frozen plastic and he'd have piles like a bunch of grapes.

Jim bumped away from the curb on frozen wheels and made an illegal left turn onto Guy Street. He switched on the radio; a choir of female voices sang the COXM time and the COXM/MOLSON BREWERY weather.

Gather up those books now and scoot right along! said the Morning Host.

"Turn that fucking thing off," said David.

Jim did not reply. He drove fast and savagely east along Sherbrooke. *You broke my heart.* The heat was beginning to come. *Tore it apart.* David could not see much; the side windows were iced over. Snow melting from his shoes. Past the *Holiday Inn.* His feet were wet. Snow was crudding up on the windshield and the wipers were frozen to the glass. Past the A&W. Great

TAKE HOME A CHUBBY CHICKEN

purple piles like a bunch of grapes. He sat staring at the translucent glass.

Cold, cold and dark. Four-thirty in the morning in Montreal. I was standing on a bank of crud left by the snow-plough. I was looking at an apartment building and wishing I was a janitor. Janitors wear warm sweaters with rocketing pheasants knitted into the back and every day they get to wash the plastic flowers in the foyer. And what they don't get is four a.m. phone calls informing them of dead bodies.

I went down the ramp at the side of the building and in through the garage. They never lock the garages. I took the elevator to the ninth, jammed the door with two paperclips, walked down to the eighth.

(The black backstrip sticking out at an angle on top of the fridge, the back of the three-ring binder. Black plastic. Both exercise-books there. The playscript and the diagrams from the last rehearsal. Coaching times for Peter and Alice. Auditorium at lunch-time.)

The piece I carry isn't elegant but it can gut-shoot a charging garbage-truck. When I stepped out on that red carpet on the eighth if anyone had said even *Boo*! I'd have blown his rocks off.

Apartment 810. The door was unlocked. I'd never seen the guy before. But someone wanted us introduced.

He'd been about fifty-five years old, a tall flabby guy with a fine appendix scar. I could tell because he hadn't got any clothes on. Some boy-scout had been writing on him with an electric barbeque-starter.

In the kitchen I found an *Odorama Air Freshener* and gave a few squirts. Even *Odorama* ("a tangy blend of citrous aromas") was better than the way *he* smelled.

His wallet was in his jacket in the bedroom. His Social Insurance and driver's licence called him Frederick Karno. I wandered out into the living room with the *Odorama* and looked along the bookcase.

> *The History of Education in Quebec*
> *The Teacher and the Law*
> *The Lamp of Learning*
> *Reader's Digest Condensed Books*
>   (Seven volumes)

I checked inside the books and on every flyleaf I read: F. Karno. In a drawer in the table I found headed notepaper:

> *Merrymount High School*
> *Principal: F. Karno (B. Comm.).*

I looked down and studied F. Karno (B. Comm.). His dentures lay on the rug. I figured he'd died of shock. Down his chest and stomach, the Barbeque-Boy had seared the words,

> *Vita brevis, ars longa*

The lettering was neater than could have been expected.

I checked the time: nearly five.

"Teacher," I said, as I closed the door behind me, "you're going to be late for school."

Mrs. Crowhurst?

Yes?

Andy Andrews calling. COXM's *Morning Host.*

No! No, it isn't!

Yes, Ma'am! Andy in person.

Oh, I can't believe it!

Yes, Ma'am. And I'm calling to play the Wondermart Goodies Game.

Oh, Mr. Andrews, I can't believe it's really you!

Ready for the first question, Mrs. Crowhurst? What is the name of Canada's biggest river?

I always watch you in the afternoons when you're the Spy in the Sky. I always wave, you know, when the helicopter comes over my house. From the balcony.

Tomorrow, David promised himself, Gruppenfuhrer McPhee would get his. But for the Gruppenfuhrer it was going to be extraordinarily painful. His arms strapped to his sides with hot hard-boiled eggs nesting in his armpits, piano wire on the thumbs, possibly electrodes on his majogglers.

"What you say?" said David.

"I said, 'Don't admit anything.' The burden's on them."

David realized the car had stopped. He gathered up the sliding pile of exercise-books and opened the car door.

"Three-thirty, then," said Jim.

"O.K. See you."

"And don't let the buggers grind you down."

It had stopped snowing. David stood for a moment watching the *Volkswagen* down the road. Piles of white exhaust hung behind it at the stop sign. Jim roared away round the corner. David turned then and crossed the road to the school.

Rising by the side of the front steps a flagpole, the Maple Leaf snapping at the steel sky. Every day at eight and four the flag was raised and lowered by the janitor, an insane Greek. Straight lines, acres of glass, neat brick. Merrymount High.

David hurried round to the side entrance. He was already twelve minutes late. A dribble of kids.

Hi, sir!

You're late, sir!

You'll get a detention, Mr. Appleby.

Ho, bloody, ho.

Within the glass doors,

    McPHEE.

Already seen. Too late to go round the front. Suspended before getting into the classroom? Prevention of moral contamination. The little shit stood only two feet higher than the REMOVE YOUR RUBBERS sign.

David climbed the steps towards him.

Back turned to McPhee, he knocked the snow off his shoes against the top step.

He still hadn't bought rubbers. They looked so ugly. Only old people in England, eccentric people wore galoshes. They were like the *Canada Tire* sign; another of his symbols of foreignness.

He pushed open the outer door.

"Good morning, Mr. McPhee."

McPhee nodded.

"It's a cold one today," said David.

Glinty eyes behind his rimless glinty glasses.

"Had trouble starting the car," said David.

Gestapo dwarf.

"The battery."

"Your class is waiting for you, Mr. Appleby," said McPhee.

He walked past McPhee, conscious of the ferrety eyes on his back, conscious that the eyes were noting the trail of ice and water melting from his shoes. Between the gleaming rows of lockers . . . *he was through . . . he was safe . . . at best she hadn't phoned at all . . .* past the A.Y. Jackson in bleary reproduction . . . *at worst she'd phoned but they knew they couldn't pin it on him . . .* past the Book Stockroom. . . .

"Mr. Appleby!"

Against the light from the glass doors McPhee was a black shape.

"Don't forget to record your late arrival in the Office!"

Foot braced against the staffroom door to give him a start, he launched himself in an *entrechat* towards the men's cloakroom. He was through. He made an Italian gesture at the mirror. He was safe. He chucked his jacket onto a peg.

As he looked into the mirror and combed his hair, the drums pointed. The Maple Leaf fluttered against a steel sky. The Gruppenfuhrer stepped forward from the silent ranks and ripped off the Lamp of Learning Award (Bronze with Acanthus Leaves). As the assembled staff chanted *You Have Broken Your Sacred Trust,* Fred Karno mumbled *in loco parentis* and snapped the symbolic stick of chalk.

He felt sorry for McPhee. Not *possibly* electrodes on his majogglers. *Definitely.* And up his arse as well.

In the deserted staff common room David waltzed around the coffee tables and sang to the plastic palm tree in its tub.

Outside the Office, he glanced at the trophy showcase crammed with gross cups and shields for Hockey, Football, Basketball, Jockstrappery in general. And the egg-cup sized thing in the back for Academic Excellence.

"*Good*morning!" cried David.

"You'll be wanting the Black Book," twinkled Miss Burgeon, the Lady Vice-Principal. Miss Burgeon did not have breasts; she had a bosom. Her dumpy body was covered by a green frock. Pinned on the bosom was a diamanté butterfly. Her glitter-framed glasses hung on chains.

"Time in this column, name in this, and reason for lateness in this," she said, pointing with her bright red fingernail.

The arid old cow was probably having a rest after suspending the day's quota of non-regulation-shade blouses, short skirts, lipsticks, all the lovely juicy-thighed girls she could get her claws into. She fluttered at her hair as he wrote.

"How do you spell 'diarrhea'?" said David.

Climbing the stairs to his classroom on the second floor, he thought of the puddle of brown water where he had stood in the Office. The word *rubbers* was still disturbing; he couldn't say it easily. It reminded him of the girl in the red linen blouse. Stained darker red under her arms with sweat. Ninety-five degrees that day and humid as a bathroom.

Ramses in Canada; not *Durex*. He didn't like asking for *Ramses*; it sounded boastful.

The girl in the red linen blouse, a stranger, a friend of a friend, had met them at the docks. Lugging suitcases in that incredible sticky heat.

"Just you wait till the winter comes," she had said. "You'll really need your rubbers then."

In the roaring canyon of Ste. Catherine Street, in the heat and sunlight, strangers in a strange land, Jim and he had looked at each other in wild surmise.

He could hear the uproar from his classroom at the other end of the corridor. He tried to remember which class it was. *Julius Caesar.* The Grade Ten mob.

He walked into the classroom and quieted the racket. He lifted the intercom phone from its rest, turned it upside down and replaced it; then he muffled the whole apparatus with his jacket so that the Office couldn't call him or listen to what he was doing.

"Your homework was to . . .?"

"Paraphrase 'O pardon me'," said Marion.

"Yes," said David.

"Act III. Scene i," said Nelson.

"Thank you," said David. "Yes, Charles?"

"It's elections, sir. Can we do them in English this morning?"

"Elections?" said David.

"I've got to run them for the King and Queen, sir. It's official."

"King and Queen?" said David.

"The Winter Carnival. I'm Grade Ten Rep on the Social Committee, sir."

"Social Committee," said David.

"O.K.? O.K. sir?"

"And this is official is it?"

"It's on the Bulletin, sir."

He'd forgotten again to pick up a copy from the counter in the Office. He took the Bulletin that Olsen offered and looked over the smudgy purple print. Basketball. Detentions. Winter Carnival Elections. He nodded and pushed back his chair. He propped himself in the corner against the window ledge.

Winter Carnival Elections. Suspensions for Gum Chewing. Play Rehearsal. Tunics to Bisect the Knee.

He looked up, gazing at the boy's back; he did not listen as the boy talked. "Chuck" Olsen. His jacket a green, blue and black tartan. Electing the King and Queen. Charles Olsen in his tartan jacket who had visited Expo 67 thirty-four times and had his "passport" stamped at every pavilion.

He heard the word "freshette."

The radiator was getting too hot against his legs. He turned round and stood gazing out of the window, his fingers slipping over the smooth red tile of the sill, across the slight roughness of the join, across to the next tile.

Directly below him in the yard, Miss Graves was blowing a whistle and waving her arms. She was wearing a pleated tunic, sturdy knockers, suet thighs. The track-suited chorus line facing her was shaking green powder-puff things to left and right.

And presumably chanting.

The whiteness of their breath hung in the air.

Give us an M!

O pardon me, thou bleeding piece of earth,

Give us an E!

That I am meek and gentle with these butchers . . .

Give us an R!

A long blast on the whistle and the chorines dropped on one knee, left arms outstretched, the green powder-puffs susurrating.

YEA, MERRYMOUNT!

Peep!

Peep!

Peep!

The girls, one after another, were jumping up into the air. Why, he wondered, were they not in the gym, why were they jumping about outside? The carnival, perhaps. Perhaps the gymnasium was being readied for this bloody carnival thing.

Did Miss Graves not feel the cold?

Could we – well, could we try . . .?

Try what?

You'll think me . . . well . . .

No. Not at all.

It's always been a desire of mine . . .

You need feel no shame, Miss Graves.

Well, if you lay on your back – yes, like that. And I stood over here – and with a backward somersault and knees bend. . . .

Miss Graves! There are limits.

Must I plead with you, Mr. Appleby?

The landing, Miss Graves! Consider the effects of an ill-judged landing.

"Can you do what?"

"Go to the other homerooms."

"That's official, too, is it?"

"It's on the Bulletin, sir."

"Right. The rest of you, *Caesar*. Act III Scene i."

David sat down at his desk and while the kids found the right place in the book stared at the framed coloured photographs of the Queen and the Duke of Edinburgh.

"Peter. Let's make up for lost time. 'Thou bleeding piece of earth.' Let's start there."

"I forgot my book in my locker, sir."

"Mary?"

"He's bleeding where they stabbed him."

"Yes, but 'earth'? Umm?"

Norovicki's face disappearing behind a large pink bubble which he deflated and engulfed again.

"Yes, Marjorie?"

"He's lying in such a lot of blood it looks like the earth is bleeding."

David shook his head.

"Support the Work of the Red Cross," said a poster at the back of the room.

"Yes, Ronnie?"

"Why couldn't he say what he meant, sir? I mean, if he's so good how come you can't understand him?"

Chapter Two

Susan's teddy blouse white against the dark heap of the navy-blue tunic crumpled on the floor; her black bra abandoned over the chair-back. The blankets were rucked at the bed's foot, the loose sheet covering her legs. The glow of the single-bar electric fire turned the room into a cave. She gathered her long black hair from the pillow, swept it back gold bracelets jingling.

"I don't know about lions," she said. "They're a bit *English*."

"You've got to have lions. Couchant."

"Trees are good, though," she said. "On both sides of the drive."

"Poplars," said David.

"Maples."

" 'My aspens dear, whose airy cages quelled, quelled or quenched in leaves the leaping sun.' "

"What are aspens?"

"Poplars."

David's fingertip traced the swell of her hip, the honey skin, the gold of Gauguin.

"Who wrote that?"

"Hopkins."

" 'Airy cages'," she said. "I like that. That's the tall ones."

Black eye-shadow, enormous dark eyes.

Kohl-darkened eyes, gold ornaments on the light gold body lit by the flames, the gleam of pearls, turning, turning, the throb and patter

31

of fingers over the skin of the derbecki, the shrill urging of the oud.

"And deer," she said. "Wild. In the woods behind the house. They'd come down in the dawn to raid the garden."

"What about bears?" said David. "I like bears."

"You've got to have blueberries for bears."

"O.K. We'll have blueberries."

"Bears that eat blueberries do little piles of blue turds."

"Polar bears have got blue tongues," said David. "Remember that one at Granby Zoo?"

She leaned towards him and tugged at the hair on his chest with her lips.

"And an old tumble-down barn," she said. "With a work place in it and lots of rusty boxes full of nails and screws and *things*."

"Linseed oil," said David.

"And wood-shavings."

"I'm not much good at wood-work," David said.

"Well we could just go in there and *touch* things. My uncle used to have a place like that in St. Jean."

"Log fires, though," said David.

"And long cords of wood stacked behind the house."

She stirred, shifted her legs.

"If you do that," she said, "I can't concentrate."

"Mmmm."

From the living room, they could hear the sounds, the click, click, click, click, the ratchet pull of the handle of Jim's adding-machine as he worked on the raw material of his thesis, stacks of bundled report cards. He was compiling the marks scored by each student during each of the four years of high school in each subject and correlating the arithmetic mean with the score attained on the provincial matriculation exam. He suspected a positive correlation.

"Can you plant *moss*?" said Susan.

Her hair tickled his face.

"Mmmm."

She rolled over onto her back, kicking off the sheet, pulling him over across her.

"You're really asking for it," she said.

"I know."

His lips brushed her dark, stiff nipples.

"Do you think it's good for old men to do it twice?" she breathed into his ear.

"Don't be cheeky."

"Cheeky," she said, gripping his buttocks.

Her hair was spread over the pillow. *Straw Hat*. Her body smelled musky.

"Why are you laughing?" he whispered.

"The springs."

Wild counterpoint of bedsprings and adding-machine, the knock of the bed's headboard against the wall. CRACK and the blind shot up.

"Oh, Jesus Christ!" said David.

"Lovely. Don't stop!"

"The Scots lady!"

"Jealous!"

Lying back in the propped pillow, the ashtray on Susan's stomach, they watched the curling smoke rise, their bodies sticky with sweat. Wind shivered the blind. The electric fire was making sizzling noises. Without the fire, purchased by Susan, love-making had been an ordeal. The heat supplied by Monsieur Gagnon caused goose-bumps. Jim's adding-machine was clicking in the living room.

"Isn't balling *good*?" said Susan.

"I wish you wouldn't *use* expressions like that," said David.

"Why? You say 'fuck' and 'screw' and . . ."

"Yes, but not . . . *here*."

"You're funny," she said.

She turned his wrist to look at his watch.

"I'm supposed to be at a movie with Frances. We went straight from school so I'd better leave soon."

She sat up in bed and David ran his finger down over the knobbles of her spine. He started humming. She twisted round and looked at him.

"Have I got a spot coming on my chin?" she said.

"It's a bit red."

"It always comes when I'm going to get my period."

"Good old spot," said David.

"Does it make me ugly?"

"Course not."

"Really?"

"Really."

He sat up, kissed her chin, and fell back onto the pillow.

"Why are you smiling?" she said.

She touched the creases at the sides of his mouth, smoothed his eyebrows.

"Umm?"

"Feel good," he said.

"Do you still love me with spots?"

"Especially with spots."

He started humming again – and then ascended into song.

> *. . . . . . . I'll not want,*
> *He makes me down to lie.*

And Susan, kneeling on the bed, her hair down over one shoulder, sang a high descant.

> *In pastures green He leadeth me,*
> *The quiet waters by.*

"For *Christ's* SAKE!" yelled Jim from the living room.

Their voices, bass and soaring, sang

> *And in my Father's house, alway,*
> *My* DWELLING-PLACE SHALL BE!

Chapter
Three

Only the monitor was in the library. She was shelving books from the trolley she pulled after her. David wished she'd hurry up; he didn't want to miss his coffee. He pretended to be searching through the literature section. A tatty and disgraceful offering but it contained most of the standard authors in standard editions. *The Oxford Book of English Verse* – the familiar dark blue cloth, gilt title. India-paper editions of the Romantics – Blake, Byron, Wordsworth, Coleridge, Keats. Apart from Masefield, Dylan Thomas, and the *Faber Book of Twentieth Century Verse,* the twentieth century might not have happened.

Would she *never* turn the corner?

It was typical of Mrs. Lewis' individualistic approach to have combined Dewey 800, 810, 820 and 890 under 800.

David rippled his fingertip over the spines. *Faber and Faber.* You could open them at any page and tell them by the design, the beauty of the type-face. *Faber.* He remembered how as a child he had been impressed by the publication date being in Roman numerals; how he had refused to learn them, preferring the foreignness, the mystery.

One Christmas he had cried onto a book, his tears splotching paler spots and streaks on the dark blue cover. He would not be comforted until his father had promised him a new copy.

Even before the words had shone and blossomed, before the wonderful figures filled his head – the Dog With Eyes Like Saucers,

Robin Hood, Long John Silver, Quartermain and Gagool, Fagin and Bumble, The Scarlet Pimpernel – he had loved the books they lived in.

A familiar ochre dust-jacket. A book by "Q".

In his father's tobacco smelling study, that book had been on the second shelf near the door above the Dickens and Conrad. He sat on the fringed carpet, his father behind him clicking and clacking at the typewriter. What might "Q" mean? What secrets hid behind that heavy black letter with its graceful, curling tail?

He saw again the loops and scrawl of his childish handwriting as it scored its way down flyleaf after flyleaf.

> *David Appleby,*
> *45 Cherville Avenue,*
> *Southbourne,*
> *Hampshire,*
> *England.*

And then?

The sound of the books thumping onto the shelves was hollow, more distant.

> *The World.*

David smiled at the ochre jacket, the thick down-strokes of the Q.

> *The Universe.*

> *The Solar System.*

He looked round and realized that the girl had turned the corner. The minute-hand of the electric clock jumped forward; the minutes of recess were slipping away.

Mrs. Lewis, an inveterate buyer of Sets and Complete Works, a devotee of fat Anthologies and Publishers' Remainders, a faithful consumer of the products of Time-Life Inc., always headed the recess coffee rush. She would now be ensconced in the most comfortable chair in the staffroom detailing the state of her rheumatism, the aches, the throbs, the twinges, the seizures, and delivering to some unfortunate an account of the bodily currents which ran between the pure copper bracelets on her left wrist and right ankle.

David slipped behind the counter and looked over the newly arrived pile. The novels were still to come in. She'd been at it again –

The World's Greatest Speeches, Favourite Stories for Every Girl and Boy, Great Canadian Disasters – but he found four of the poetry books he'd entered on the Suggestions List. They were unstamped. He took them and slipped out.

He hurried down the stairs and along to the staffroom where he stashed the books in his cloakroom locker. He stole books from the library regularly and gave them to Susan and the three students in his grade eleven classes who read.

In the crowded Common Room, he took a cup and saucer from the counter and joined the queue. Above the coffee urn hung one of Eaton's Canadian landscapes. Spring, Summer, and Fall decorated the other walls.

"You remember our little conversation last week. . . ."

"Pardon?"

"Well," said Mrs. Gowly, "she *still* hasn't given me her set of *Moonfleet* and it's three weeks now."

David tut-tutted.

"And her class are doing *Sunshine Sketches* now. I enquired. *And* she's still got *Cue for Treason*. I mean, we do have schedules. It just isn't reasonable. And the trouble – my husband brought home a roll of wallpaper and I had my class cover those *Cue for Treason* and I'm informed *she* made *her* class tear the covers off."

David shook his head.

"And they've got to read it in time for the Easter exam."

"Exactly," said David, "exactly."

He had to tip the urn towards him to get any coffee out; it smelled bitter. He took a spoon from the saucer of a used cup and Mr. Weiss passed him the milk jug.

"Not, of course, that she hasn't every right," said Mrs. Gowly.

"Sorry?"

"To tear the covers off. But they *are* a protection. That's what *I* don't understand."

"Quite," said David.

Garry was waving him over.

"If you'll excuse me," he smiled. "Mr. Westlake seems to . . ."

Garry squeezed up on the long couch making room at the end. David took one of Garry's cigarettes from the packet on the coffee-table.

"Grierson wants to see us at twelve-thirty," said Garry. "We'll have to cancel the rehearsal."

"What's he want to see us for?"

"He didn't say. I just saw him in the corridor."

"In his office?"

"Yes, something about the play, I expect."

Oafish Hubnichuk came over and started bellowing into the wall-phone, his vast buttocks inches from David's head. David glared up at Hubnichuk's back, at Hubnichuk's height and bulk.

WHAT? WELL, HE PICKED UP AN ASSIST. YEAH. FROM THE BLUE LINE.

"Can you get one of the kids to put up a notice on the auditorium?" said Garry. "I'm teaching till twelve-thirty and I've got to get some maps now for next period."

"Ah!" said David. "From the 'Communications Resource Centre'."

YEAH! WHEN HE WENT UP THE LEFT BOARDS. YEAH! YEAH!

They stared at Hubnichuk.

"I hope Grierson isn't going to quibble. . . ."

YOU PUT YOUR MONEY ON THE LEAFS!

"I didn't hear that," said Garry, "because MR. HUBNICHUK IS SHOUTING."

Hubnichuk looked round and winked.

"Hope he isn't going to quibble about the money for the sets," said David, "because I ordered the timber from *Pascal's* last week."

"Shouldn't think so," shrugged Garry.

"By the way," said David, "the phantom raider struck again this morning. Liberated four more."

GRARF, GRARF laughed Hubnichuk.

"Cummings, Auden, Layton, and a new Ted Hughes."

Garry smiled and shook his head.

"If they catch you, you'll never win the Lamp of Learning Award, you know."

"Gives you pause, that," said David. "Leave me a couple of cigarettes, will you?"

NOT A CHANCE! HE'S GOOD FOR YEARS YET!

He moved further up the couch away from Hubnichuk's looming bulk.

Near the door, Garry was buttonholed by Mr. Follet, his department head. Garry smiled, nodded, said something. Follet chortled. David watched the play of expressions on Garry's face. How pale he was! When he was emphasizing, he always ran his fingers through his short, straw-coloured hair. During rehearsals he became a different person, the lick of hair curling down into his eyes, furiously thrust back only to fall again and again as he gestured and shouted in mottled rage. Follet listening now, smoothing his ghastly Chaplin moustache with a deliberate thumb.

David felt a surge of affection for Garry as he watched them; humiliating that a man like Garry should have to take direction from that pompous, flatulent little crapper, the vile Follet who had once seriously referred to Shakespeare as "The Swan of Avon."

Apart from Miss Leet, who favoured Ayn Rand, Garry was the only teacher in the school who read books. They had discovered each other about a month after David's arrival the previous year. He couldn't remember how, exactly, but he remembered their circlings, their probings into who liked what, who had read this, seen that – the conversations becoming warmer and more intimate as they discovered common enthusiasms for "Carry On" films, Evelyn Waugh, Ingmar Bergman, and Nathaniel West. Garry had given him Ring Lardner. Difficult, too, to say when, exactly, they had stopped fencing and posing – perhaps after the Dashiell Hammett *vs* Raymond Chandler argument. Perhaps after the evening last winter David had persuaded him to go to the *Esquire Show Bar* to hear Howling Wolf.

GRARF, GRARF

June had been in hospital that week and they'd stayed up half the night. That was the night the drunk in *Champ's* had said to the manager, "Who do you think you are? King Shit of Piss Island? Eh? King Shit of the Yukon?"

And then they'd tamped down the drink with food somewhere

and somehow they'd been driving past the headquarters of the Board and Garry had stopped and they'd climbed the steps, treading into the new snow, and pissed together on the big brass doors.

Snowing heavily and Garry had flung out an arm and thundered to the cars labouring past below,

Who are these who thus against
Our portals . . .

and David, drink and happiness inspired, had said,

. . . do, intemperate, urinate?

He wondered if Follet would believe that the almost boyish figure in front of him, charming, neat and energetic-looking in slacks and sports jacket, delivered murderous imitations – Follet lamenting the decline of standards and the barbarian without the gate, Follet deploring the Canadian monotone as compared with the instrumental beauty of English voices, Follet excoriating the intellectual paucity of Canadian universities, Follet confidentially deploring the presence in Montreal of vast numbers of those of the "Hebrew persuasion."

It was Garry who had saved him from Follet on numerous occasions last year; whenever Follet threatened inspections of David's Canadian History class, Garry had prepared the lessons. It was Garry, ten years older than David, who listened to his complaints, commiserated, offered advice. It was Garry who lent him money to fly to England when his mother was ill; Garry who talked him out of his more risky schemes of revenge and retaliation.

But their friendship, now, he realized, was slowly becoming confined to school, to occasional parties, to those few times Garry could get away for a beer. His visits to the house, invitations to dinner, were dropping off. June and Chrissy were becoming a restraint between them, a subject they rarely mentioned.

He wished he could like the ghastly June but she was making it increasingly clear that she regarded him as an enemy, as a force which pulled Garry back towards enthusiasms, late hours, and drinking. She'd been particularly annoyed about their producing the play; after one long rehearsal recently she'd managed to forgive him for about two hours for spilling a drink and treading on Chrissy's *Cat-in-a-Boat.*

Follet clapped Garry on the shoulder and did his jocund chortle again.

The obscene little rotundity.

He was certain they could work Sir Charles Pharco-Hollister on Follet but Garry kept saying that it needed more careful planning and preparation. He'd done some preliminary work the week before, alluding to a non-existent historical journal,

". . . a rather fascinating theory in the O.N.Q."

"The . . . . . . ?"

"Oxford Notes and Queries."

which had discussed new rumours of Queen Victoria's bastard son. There was mentioned the possibility of his having been sent to Canada. Family papers recently and fortuitously discovered at Harewood House.

"Good Lord! That'd shake the old dovecots up a bit," Follet had said.

The word "Oxford" alone had him hooked.

Some of the staff were sure that Garry would be made the next head of the history department when Follet retired at the end of the year.

Mr. Weinbaum had been talking to Mr. Healey, David remembered, last year, last summer when the promotions and transfers were posted on the Principal's Notice Board.

"Westlake'll get History," Weinbaum had said. "You watch him go. This time next year – just see if I'm not right."

Everyone was in shirtsleeves and drinking Cokes. Lunchtime. A loud bridge postmortem going on at the table near the window.

Mr. Healey, the woodwork man, was short, fiercely contained. He had come from Yorkshire originally where silence is equated with profundity. Mr. Healey had considered Mr. Weinbaum's remark.

(He was reputed to burst into the girls' shower-room from time to time, shouting,

"Is there someone in here smoking?")

After a long pause, he said,

"I've seen several like him in my years with the Board."

And long seconds later,

"Principals now, most of 'em."

NOT A CHANCE!

And not a moment too soon if Garry did get it. The abominable Follet issued mimeograph lists at the beginning of each term detailing which pages of the history books should be studied and which should be omitted, the division based on his crafty study of previous provincial exams. Although from Ontario, he called England "The Old Country" or, if he was in military mood, "Blighty." His fondest and most frequently recalled memories were of wartime Cockney humour, Picadilly Circus, Bayswater, and London whores whom he referred to as "girlies."

Garry had created Sir Charles Pharco-Hollister about seven years ago when he had been teaching in Vancouver but Sir Charles had become a monster grown out of control. They spent hours in elaborating him, composing his *bons mots,* his ripostes, his eccentricities, the titles of his books. They both taught about him, David going so far as to dictate notes.

Sir Charles, depending on the class taught, was military governor of Fort Pharco in Alberta, a Father of Confederation, or one of the Fredericton poets. He was variously alcoholic, incestuous, syphilitic, a scalper of Indians, a bastard son of Queen Victoria and her Scots gillie. Dark rumours circulated about the exact nature of his relationship with "Bliss" Carman. In British Columbia, he had lent his name to the turbulent Pharco River.

YEAH! ON THE POWER PLAY. NO! IN THE FIRST PERIOD.

David longed to work the whole job on Follet, to skilfully play him towards the landing-net; but what the shape of that net might be he couldn't quite grasp. An exposure perhaps, a chastising, a ridicule, or perhaps the pleasure lay only in the performance?

YOU CAN BET YOUR GOODIES ON THAT!

Hubnichuk's sausage fingers were scratching his behind.

TRADE HIM? NEVER!

Who but Hubnichuk would wear a black suit, black shoes, and *white socks?*

Six feet three and podgy, podgy hands, vast moonlike Ukrainian face, his fleshy Ukrainian neck bulging over his collar.

The Boor No. 666 of Merrymount High.

Hubnichuk – half-time gym teacher and half-time Guidance Counselor.

Mens sana (a.m.) in corpore sano (p.m.).

Hubnichuk always winked at him. Hubnichuk called him "Davy." Hubnichuk had even slapped him on the back.

At every encounter, ten times a day, in the corridor, in the staff-room, in the office, on the stairs, Hubnichuk said either,

> *What's the good word, Davy-boy?*

or,

> *What do you say, Dave?*

One of these days Hubnichuk was going to push him too far. Instead of a polite smile, a polite mumble, he would round on him.

> *What do I say?*
>
> *What do I say, Mr. Hubnichuk?*
>
> *I say, Mr. Hubnichuk, that you are a hulking, mannerless oaf and that I would be vastly obliged, if, in future, you did not presume to address me by my Christian name.*
>
> YEAH!
>
> GRARF, GRARF.
>
> YEAH! WILL DO.

Mr. Hubnichuk clanged down the phone, bent, and squeezed David's knee painfully. He winked.

"The wife," he said.

J. D. Grierson (B. Comm.), the principal of Merrymount High, sat behind the shining expanse of his desk-top. His head was centred between two complimentary calendars on the wall behind, one from the *Bank of Montreal*, the other from the *Canadian Imperial Bank of Commerce.*

He waved a hand and Garry and David sat down.

The desk-top was empty except for a copy of *Night Haul* and a green marble block into which were spiked three pens.

He held up the copy of the play.

Maritime and stolid, chewing at the insides of his cheeks, he looked at them in turn.

"I'm surprised at you, Mr. Westlake," he said, "You're older than Mr. Appleby here. You've been teaching longer. I'd have thought you'd have had more sense."

He tossed the book onto the desk-top.

"The school has received a phone-call," he said. "From an agitated parent; from a *distressed* parent."

He looked from one to the other.

"Complaining of filthy language in this play."

Garry and David glanced at each other.

"I looked the play over" – his big hands wrapped the book into a cylinder and then released it, pages riffling – "and was disturbed by what I found."

He opened the book and turned a few pages, shaking his head. He took off his glasses. There was a click and slight rattle as he placed them on the desk. David stared at the warped book, the creased front cover.

"You have made a serious error of judgement," said Grierson.

"I don't know exactly what language you're referring to, Mr. Grierson," said David, "but surely . . ."

"Mr. Appleby! Even someone with your limited teaching experience shouldn't need instruction in what is acceptable, what is in good taste."

"But in the context, the language is an expression of character. It's natural for those characters to talk in that way."

"A school can't encourage this sort of thing. A play, Mr. Appleby, should be a cultural event."

"But when you use the word 'cultural' to . . ."

"I'm not interested in contexts, Mr. Appleby, and I'm not interested in what is natural. I'm interested in the good name and reputation of Merrymount High."

He cleared his throat and consulted his watch.

"I have a meeting at one o'clock," he said. "I'd like to see a copy of the play – tomorrow or Friday, say – with those words taken out."

"You want us to bowdlerize the whole thing," said David.

"No," said Grierson, getting up from behind his desk, "I want it cleaned up and those words cut out."

He walked over with them to the door.

More cheek-chewing.

"We have to remember," he said, "that we're public servants. We have a responsibility to our students, to the Board, to the wider community."

He opened the door.

"Surprised, Mr. Westlake."

The door closed behind them.

"Dear God!" said David, breaking into their silence again. "Public fucking servants!"

Garry shrugged.

"Let's go and see if there's any sandwiches left," he said.

They walked along the corridor from the staffroom and started down the stairs towards the roar of the basement cafeteria.

"What an ignorant, mindless fucking *get* that man is!"

"That's a new one," said Garry.

"Hold him up to the light – not a brain in sight!"

"Get?"

"Oh. It's short for 'whore's get' – that which a whore has begat."

"The preferred Canadian is 'hoor'."

"Whoremonger!" said David. "Whore*master*! And there's many a true word spoke in jest."

"I wonder when he learned 'wider community'?" said Garry.

"Perhaps the Board gives Principal-Lessons," said David.

"It does make you wonder how he ever got there," said Garry. "Even when you know."

"Education's First Law, mate. That's how. Shit floats."

"There's only bologna left," said the cafeteria woman triumphantly. "Or *May Wests.*"

"He probably came in after the war," said Garry. "All the less dim ones had been killed."

"The *slightly* less dim ones," said David.

The Staff Dining Room was empty except for Miss Oldane. Miss Oldane taught Geography and Health and Welfare in grades eight and nine. She carried a tiny pearl-handled fruit knife in her purse with which she peeled her recess and lunchtime apples.

Her first Health and Welfare lesson of each year to the new grade eight girls advised them *never* to put bus-tickets between their lips if their hands were full with books, purses, and gloves because bus-drivers had been known to touch – to scratch . . . well . . . their *private parts.*

Garry and David ignored her, sat down. David peeled open his bologna sandwich and lathered it with mustard.

"Still," said Garry, splitting open his carton of milk, "maybe we ought to think about it."

"I thought we were agreed. *I'll* write it. And tastefully nasty it'll be, too."

"Wasted on Grierson."

"Well I'll enjoy it anyway – and he'll catch the drift."

"Maybe we really ought to consider going on with it, David."

"What do you mean?"

"Well," said Garry. "I don't know. I've been thinking about it and of course we're right – I don't mean that, but I've been thinking about the kids. They've been working hard for months – I just feel we can't pull the rug out – BAM! I don't really know if we've any *right* to do that."

"Oh, bullshit! We can tell them what happened and . . ."

"Yes, but is it *fair?* Fair to them. And would they really be able to understand why it's important?"

"Why not? They're not stupid."

"Yes, but they're young and from *their* point of view . . ."

"Are you *serious?*"

"Some of them'll just see it as a squabble between us and Grierson."

"They can see us doing something on principle. *That's* important. And if some of them don't really understand, that's not *our* responsibility."

"That's what I'm trying to get at, David. Don't you understand? It's fine for *us*, but I really don't know how far we ought to let our *own* feelings . . ."

"For Christ's sake! Look at what we'd be left with! The weirdest café in the western world – *I say, mind what you're doing with that jolly frying-pan!*"

"Oh, come on! You're exaggerating and . . ."

"*I'm* not cutting the balls off it!"

Miss Oldane snapped her purse shut and walked out.

"And *that*," said David, "is the *whole* point."

"I don't think it is – no."

"Oh?"

"I'm *trying*," said Garry, "*trying* to suggest that being black and white about it isn't really . . ."

"Pass the mustard, will you?"

"Isn't really being honest with our particular situation."

David bit into his sandwich and then opened it up again to sprinkle pepper on the mustard.

"I really hate bologna," he said. "You need this to mask the taste."

"Neat and over-simple," said Garry.

David shrugged.

"Another thing," said Garry, "another complication – quite apart from the kids. We've got to live and work in this place. A lot of people have put their own time into this. How are *they* going to feel? And I mean *feel*. Try explaining moral problems to Mrs. Kinsella!"

"Sounds 'public servantish' to me," said David.

"What *would* you say to Mrs. Kinsella? And to Healey?"

"If they don't understand, that's *their* problem. Fuck 'em."

Garry nodded.

"Easy, isn't it?" he said. "So simple."

"Exactly," said David.

"And selfish," said Garry.

David shrugged.

"It's the best I can do," he said. "And meanwhile, you go on and Grierson rides again."

"*Aren't* we being fastidious!" said Garry.

"I try to be," said David.

"In this particular context, I think you're wrong, David. You've got to . . ."

"I haven't *got* to do *anything*. If you want to sell the play out, you go ahead."

"But you're prepared to 'sell' the kids out?"

David got up and dropped the crumpled napkin onto his plate.

"If you like," he said. "I think I'm doing them a favour."

He pushed in his chair.

"I didn't see *you* saying much to Grierson in there," he said.

"Now you're getting *really* pleasant," said Garry.

David shrugged.

"You think we were called in there to *discuss* something?" demanded Garry. "I didn't say anything because there wasn't any point in saying anything."

"We should have told him to go fuck himself," said David.

"Oh, don't be so ballsachingly *adolescent!*" snapped Garry.

"We should have told him to go fuck himself."

"One of these days," said Garry, "you're going to learn."

"We should have told him to go fuck himself," said David.

Garry closed up the empty milk carton, pinching the waxed cardboard edges together, scoring the sides of the crease with his thumb-nail.

"We should talk about it, David."

"There isn't anything to say."

48

David walked out through the kitchen and made his way through the mob of kids in the cafeteria.

In the Men's Staffroom, Henry Jockstrap was arm-wrestling with another oaf; Mr. Margolis was talking about his pension; Mr. Renfrew was reading the answers in the back of the grade ten algebra text; Mr. Bardolini was extolling to Mr. Healey the virtues of the *Wonder Book of Universal Knowledge* which he sold on commission in the evenings to local parents.

The washroom was empty. He looked down to see if there were feet showing under any of the lavatory doors. He studied his face in the mirror as he combed his hair. He washed his hands in scalding water and dried them on the roller towel, yanking length after echoing length from the machine. The urinal gurgled and then gushed water for a few seconds from the green copper nozzles at the top of each stall.

He looked out over the white-painted glass on the bottom part of the high window. It was snowing again, light flakes drifting. The air was yellow with the gloom of a storm. Goal-posts stuck black out of the snow-covered playing field. Just below in the yard, three men in overcoats were standing round Mr. Cherton's new *Sting Ray*. Mr. Davidson. Mr. Monpetit. The flow of water gurgled back into silence.

David mounted the stand and stood in the middle of the three stalls. He unzipped his trousers. Rubber footsteps squelched in the cloakroom. The swing-door banged open and Hubnichuk came in. They nodded. Hubnichuk was wearing a shabby blue track-suit.

He mounted the stand to David's left. Standing back, he pulled down the elastic front of his trousers. He cradled his organ in the palm of his hand; it was like a three-pound eye-roast. Suddenly, he emitted a tight, high-pitched fart, a sound surprising in so large a man.

Footsteps.

Mr. Weinbaum came in.

"So this is where the nobs hang out!" he said.

"Some of them STICK OUT from time to time!" said Hub-nichuk.

Their voices echoed.

Mr. Weinbaum mounted the stand and stood in front of the stall to David's right.

"If you shake it more than twice," he said, "you're playing with it."

Water from the copper nozzle rilled down the porcelain.

There was a silence.

David studied the manufacturer's ornate cartouche.

The Victory and Sanitary Porcelain Company.

Inside the curlicued scroll, a wreathed allegorical figure.

Victory?

Sanitation?

Mr. Weinbaum shifted, sighed.

"I got the best battery in Canada for $18.00," he said.

Chapter Four

The ice in David's glass chunked and clicked. He let the scotch wash round his mouth. He lay back in his armchair watching Jim who was sitting cross-legged on the floor surrounded by magazines and newspapers. The colours of the *Canada Tire* sign washed the window.

Jim absorbed pounds of journalism every week. He read papers and magazines on politics, finance, photography, motoring, cinema, education, true confessions, sport, scientific research, aviation and psychology; he could marshal the background to every coup, massacre, and takeover-bid; he could name obscure officials in obscure agencies and knew the meaning of each and every acronym. The thought of an unread newspaper prevented him from sleeping and every night at about eleven-thirty he bundled up and went out to buy the next day's *Gazette*.

David tipped his glass and let the ice-cubes rest against his lip. By his chair stood a freshly opened bottle of *Cutty Sark*. It was the last Friday of the month, payday. He had given Jim the rent-share, paid his half of the bills, put aside money for food and expenses, and was left with one hundred and seventy dollars. (Take off eight for the scotch – one hundred and sixty-two dollars.)

He took out his wallet and looked at the money again. One orange one, three twenties, a two, and one unexplained green one. He wondered what he could spend it on. Monopoly money. He had passed "Go" again.

Jim was always buying suits and shoes but new clothes on David looked messy within hours. Jim would have looked elegant in a sheet of newspaper.

"Jim," said David, "you're a bloody ectomorph."

"Is there legitimately a noun?" said Jim, not looking up.

"Yes," said David. "There is."

Books?

But he couldn't read more than twenty-five dollars' worth of paperbacks in a month.

Perhaps this should be the month to buy a bottle of Napoleon brandy from the QLB – the oldest they had, the seventy-five-dollar one. And then he could have a bath, wash his hair and shave, put on his best clothes, and drink it. The shirt white and slightly starched.

He leaned over the arm of the chair, grunting with the effort, and grabbed the neck of the bottle. He poured another large drink, watching the scotch spread down into the melted ice water like thinning smoke.

Salvador Dali, he remembered reading, used to dress up in eighteenth-century military uniform, epaulettes and tricorn hat, and masturbate in front of a mirror. A good man, Dali.

"Don't take your boots off!" called Jim as they heard the front door open.

David heaved himself out of the chair.

"Jim's giving us a lift," he said as he went down the hall.

Susan was holding her coat open.

"Well, just *look* at you!" he said.

"Posh, eh?" said Susan. "For going out to dinner."

"That's your 'little basic black,' is it?"

"New. Do you like it?"

David enfolded her.

"Love *it*, love *you*."

They edged down the stairs holding on to the bannister because the lights on the third and second landings were burned out. Barefoot, a comforter pinned to his undershirt, diaper sagging, one of Monsieur Gagnon's brood stood wide-eyed at the bottom of the stairs.

"Piss off, you snotty horror," said Jim.

"Jim!" said Susan.

"Once a Gagnon always a Gagnon."

"Tarred with the same brush," said David.

"Shall we breed up serpents in our bosom?" said Jim.

"Extirpate the buggers root and branch," said David.

"You're not funny," said Susan, going over to Gagnon's door. "Either of you. The poor little shit ought to be in bed. He hasn't even got socks on."

She knocked again.

Madame Gagnon opened the door about half an inch.

"Your little boy must have wandered out," said Susan.

"Monsieur not here."

"Your little boy's out here."

Madame Gagnon scooped him in and slammed the door.

"Miserable *bitch*!" shouted Susan.

In the back of the *Volkswagen*, holding Susan's hand, David could feel the workings of the scotch. The flashing neon, the thick crowds along Ste. Catherine, the sudden wink of brake-lights beyond the dim confines of the car were like a distant drive-in movie. David felt comfortable, the day receding.

He began to realize his hunger. He'd had nothing since lunch – a chopped egg sandwich and a carton of milk ruined first by Follet rumbling over the word "shit" which had miraculously slipped by in the student newspaper.

I expect they order things very differently
in the Old Country, Mr. Appleby.

Oh, indeed.

Quite. Yes.

Total lack of RESPECT.

My word, yes.

Follet had tiny feet. Follicles. Nasty twinkling shoes.

And ruined second by Hubnichuk. Eating the second half and reading a novel when Hubnichuk, *mens sana*, had sat beside him on the couch. After a few moments of breathing Hubnichuk had said,

Reading, eh?

And not even a good sandwich to start with. Too much mayonnaise.

He probably had to buy his follicles in the children's department. Good.

Susan squeezed his hand. He leaned over and kissed her.

"Italian Straw Hat," he said.

He started to think about the next drink he would have. Most probably a martini – a double martini. Very dry. Ice. Lemon peel. Susan had said once, in a bar, in the Piccadilly Bar of the Sheraton Mount Royal,

Gin tastes like Christmas trees smell.

Jim turned off Ste. Catherine onto Stanley Street and swung into the entrance of *Pigeon Hole Parking*. Three cars were lined up in front of them. Jim got out to hand in the keys at the office window. David held the seat forward for Susan to clamber out.

A voice said,

I think it's down to the left, dear.

A voice that made David turn.

McPHEE!

The tableau seared his mind like a magnesium flare over No Man's Land.

Just turning away from the office-window, McPhee with two women. One, a big woman in a fur coat. A white glove. The other in a black coat, a black evening gown down to her feet. Glitter of black sequins. McPhee in a black overcoat, glinty glasses. A little green hat with a cord round it, a tiny cockade of peacock feather in the cord. Jaunty. Alpine.

McPHEE!

The big one in the fur coat was blocking McPhee's view. David crouched, wrenched *Volks* door open, tipped front seat and scrabbled into the back, wedging himself onto the floor.

The door on the other side opened, the car swayed under someone's weight, the front seat bulged against his head. The motor started; the door slammed. The car moved forward. Sounds of metal gates folding back. The front wheels clattered over the rim of the elevator's floor, the back wheels. Handbrake. Gates sliding across. A jerk. The car was rising.

The handle of Jim's snow-shovel was sticking in his crotch. An inch from his face, the red nylon bristles of the windshield brush-and-scraper.

The light kept changing. Dark, a second or two of light, dark again. Rising through the floors.

His knee was soaked from the melted ice on the floor. The blade of the shovel was cutting into his ankle.

A jerk. Sounds of gates again. Rattle and bump over the rim. He braced himself, fingers splayed on the rubber mat, as the driver accelerated. Suddenly the brakes were jammed on, thudding him against the front seat. The engine roared and cut out. Door open, slammed. Footsteps.

David waited, feeling queasy and sobered.

He knelt and looked out of the window. Empty. He climbed out, brushing the dirt from his sleeves and trousers. He was in an echoing concrete cavern. Sodium lights. The air was thick with the stench of exhaust fumes. His footsteps sounded. He came out from between the cars and looked round for a door.

"What you doing here?"

David turned. Hand to brow, suggestive of pain and bewilderment, he said, "Where am I?"

"You supposed to get out downstairs," said the man.

David walked over towards him. He was holding a green plastic hosepipe, wearing blue overalls with the company's insignia on the bib. A pigeon looking out of a box. Curving underneath the pigeon were the words —

Service and Courtesy
The Friendly Pigeon

"You supposed to get out downstairs," repeated the man.

"I must have passed out," said David.

"Not for public here."

"I sometimes pass out. Faint."

The man looked blank.

"Unconscious," said David.

"For public is downstairs."

"I suffer from a disease," said David. "An illness."

The man stared.

"Maucomia," said David.

"Is door," said the man, pointing.

David came out through the *No Entry* and stood in the shadows looking round. He walked out onto the pavement and looked up and down the street. Susan waved to him from the doorway of a sporting-goods store across the road.

"Did he see me?"

"I don't think so. He wasn't really looking that way."

"Jesus Christ!" said David, shaking his head.

"Where have you *been*?" said Susan.

"Upstairs. Did he see *you*?"

"I turned my back and grabbed Jim. He went right past."

"Where *is* Jim?"

"Went off to a movie."

"You're *sure* he didn't see me?"

"He couldn't have."

"Jesus, that was close!" said David. "I had a very nasty time up there with a man with a green hosepipe."

Susan was shivering. She put her arms around him.

"It's O.K.," he said.

"It's not that. My bum's freezing."

"Let's go and eat then," said David.

Le Poisson D'or, a family-run restaurant with a small menu, was one of their favourite eating places. Most of the customers were regulars, men and women who worked nearby at *Radio Canada*, men who sat over their coffee reading *Le Devoir*, families. There were about twenty tables.

"Go in first and look round," said David. "I've had enough excitement and danger for one bloody evening."

"No, you."

"Put your shades on."

"No, *you* go."

After glancing round the end of the coat rack, David pulled back the window curtain and beckoned Susan in. They sat at the rear of the restaurant near the swing doors into the kitchen, a position David favoured as he could watch the to and fro of the waitresses.

He sipped the martini and read the menu. The ghastly Edith Piaf ended – all shouting and accordions – and something orchestral began. Light gleamed on copper kettles and saucepans which decorated the walls. He moved the vase of flowers to the side of the table. Susan's hair was piled up on top of her head but the word "bun" wasn't right; it suggested severity. He drained the martini and chewed the piece of lemon peel. He smiled at her.

"What if he'd seen you," she said, "and opened the car-door . . ."

"And I was grovelling on the floor . . ."

"Good-evening, Mr. Appleby!"

"Oh, Mr. McPhee! Good-evening. I'm . . . ah . . . just . . ."

The waitress brought him another drink. She was wearing a plastic slide on her blouse with MARIE printed on it – a nasty practice and something new for *Le Poisson D'or*. It probably meant that they were going to have to find a new place. Soon, middle-aged men in suits would be talking in loud voices.

Ah, thank you, Marie.

Gourmets claimed that strong drink deadened the palate. Well, balls to them. He polished off the *sardines marinés a la niçoise*.

"What are you giggling about?" he said.

"It'd have been a real *jaarustna*."

"What's that?"

"It's Arabic for 'making a spectacle of yourself'."

"It'd have been a bloody sight more than that."

"A making of shame."

"It isn't funny," said David.

"Un Grand Spectacle," said Susan.

"Tous les Soirs," said David, smiling.

He'd always enjoyed the "Grand Spectacle" signs outside the clubs and bars because underneath the flickering arrows it always said

BEER AND WINE DANCING

Like "Amateur Hour."

And now –

> *fresh from a triumphal tour of the Gaspé –*
> *that famed beer-and-wine-dancer . . . your favourite*
> *alcoholic terpsichorean . . . pissed as a newt . . .*

"Oh, and a bottle of *Moulin à Vent*, please."

"You're getting stoned," said Susan. "Why don't we have half a bottle?"

"No, I'm not. Just relaxed, that's all."

"Your eyes have gone funny."

"Nonsense! Nothing wrong with my eyes. Good enough for the Hong Kong Police Force."

"What?"

"Didn't know that, did you? I passed a medical. At least five foot eight in stocking feet, thingummy vision without glasses. Nearly went there."

"Why?"

"I don't know, really. Something to do. Answered an ad in the *New Statesman* or *Educational Supplement*. Answered one to go teaching Dyaks in Borneo, as well. But you had to go firking around in the jungle for that one."

"A policeman!"

"Oh, I don't know! You wear those shorts and knee-socks and you have a swagger-stick for poking the natives. Rather enjoyable, really."

"Don't be disgusting."

"Defending the far-flung bounds, lesser breeds and all that. Just round this lot up, Ah Sing."

"Shss!"

"What do you mean 'Shss'? There's nothing wrong with the Hong Kong Police Force. A much maligned body of men."

"David. Shut-up! People can hear you."

"I was offered one in Australia as well but there *are* limits. That ungodly bloody accent for one thing and they call you 'cobber' all the time."

"Well you call people 'mate'," said Susan.

"Not the same thing at all – oh, I'm sorry. For the lady."

"Thank you," said Susan.

"Perhaps if I move this . . ." said David.

"Merci, monsieur."

"I'm not a racist, but do you know what Australians eat for breakfast?" asked David, leaning forward. "They eat *steaks*! With fried eggs on top. Isn't that *disgusting*!"

"Your sleeve's in the mashed potato."

"I'd rather Borneo."

"Good salad," said Susan.

"Which one do you think was McPhee's wife?" said David.

"The small one."

"Bet it was the big one."

"What if neither of them was?" said Susan.

"Hey, that's *it*. He *hires* them. He dresses up like a schoolboy and they give him the strap. And they make him write out lines and essays. And he has to say, 'Please, Miss. Can I touch it?' And they – no, the big one – says, 'What a *dirty* little boy! What a *grubby* little boy! A little boy who hasn't washed his hands.' And the small one doesn't wear knickers and he sits on the floor and looks up her skirt while she reads out loud from *The Mill on the Floss*."

"Doesn't he ever *do* it?"

"Of *course* not! They just beat him up."

"Poor McPhee."

"There's no point feeling sorry for him. He *likes* it."

"Did I tell you about Brunhoff's photographs?" said Susan. "I had to go and see him again this afternoon – talking of sex maniacs."

"What for *this* time?"

"Goofing off on Tuesday and Wednesday."

" 'Goofing off'," said David.

"So?"

"Ugh. I didn't know you'd 'goofed' anyway."

"Yes, I told you – sure I did. I went to the *Elysée* on Tuesday to see the Bergman – remember? And Wednesday, Frances and I went down to the museum to see the African exhibition. The masks."

"And they copped you."

"They phoned my mother to ask if she'd written the note."

"Is *nothing* sacred?"

"*Wild Strawberries* is on again next week – we're going, eh?"

"Sure. Hey. I was meaning to ask you about that. About Brunhoff,
I mean. The latest thing on your Kardex cards says 'Suspected of
drug addiction.' What the hell did you tell him that for? They
keep all that shit and use it against you, you know."

"I didn't tell him. Mr. Cherton found me filling up an ink car-
tridge with a hypodermic we stole from biology. I guess he told him."

"What do you mean?"

"Well, instead of throwing it away you can refill it. You put the
needle through the end and when you pull it out the plastic closes
up again."

"I'd better whip that card out," said David.

"Anyway," said Susan, "we had to go together this afternoon and
he gave us one of his talks and then Fran said she was tired in
school and her work was suffering because she didn't sleep nights –
and he asked her why – and do you know what she said? She looks
right at him and she never blushes or anything and she said she
couldn't sleep because she had burning sensations between her legs."

"The poor bugger! What does he *do*?"

"He keeps polishing his glasses with little lavender papers from
a package and he says, 'I see. Yes, I see.' And his eyes are all sort
of naked looking – oyster-eyes. She goes every gym class and most
of algebra now and he says she's deeply disturbed and she can go
whenever she feels the need to talk."

"He lusts after her. Desire inflames him. She rages like a hectic
in his blood."

"He's sort of *dirty* horny," said Susan.

"He's gripped by carnal thingies," said David. "He who desires
but acts not breeds pestilence. Never trust a man who hangs a copy
of 'The Light of the World' in his office. Student Christian Movement! Brunhoff and the Spotties will now lead us in 'Guide Me, O

Thou Great Redeemer.' Guide Me, O Thou Guidance Counselor, Pilgrim in This Barren Land. Have you ever considered why student Christians are predominantly spotty?"

"Listen," said Susan. "Shut-up."

"Have you noticed that? They're very spotty."

"I want to tell you about the photographs."

"When they asked him if he'd be prepared to go on strike," said David, "he said he wouldn't because *he* served *two* masters, the Board and Our Lord."

"He's got these photographs on his desk. He's got one of his wife, and his kid, and his house, and his car and this afternoon he'd got a new one of a lot of candles."

"What do you mean 'candles'?"

"Coloured candles standing on a table. Hundreds of them."

"Lighted candles?"

"No. Just rows of them. So we asked him what it was and he said it's his hobby. He goes home every night and makes candles. Isn't that *sad*?"

"He lights them in the darkness," said David, "and the tiny flames, individually weak, combined, drive away, dispel the night of sin and ignorance whose sombre pall enshrouds . . ."

"He's creepy," said Susan. "If you don't want it, can I have your asparagus?"

"When you've eaten every last ort and scrap, would you like dessert? Coffee? Brandy?

"Just coffee. We're not going to be late, are we? I want to see both sets."

"Bags of time. Masses of time."

David put his nose down into the snifter and breathed in the fumes of the Armagnac; not a "bouquet"; definitely fumes. Gold and amber light swam in the glass. Light gleamed on the oil in the wooden salad bowl. Green, white, a piece of lettuce leaf. He warmed the glass in his hands. Somewhere in the distant noise of crockery and conversation someone was smoking a French cigarette. Susan's hair had loosened, in the light from behind a mist of hair like a halo.

The Armagnac tasted thick. Unliquid. Light lurched. After-images. He realized that he was massively, comfortably, splendidly, luxuriously and soporifically drunk. He breathed heavily into the glass. The rim, he discovered, was hurting his nose.

"Something dreadful must be wrong," he said, having been brooding about it, "if they're willing to pay your fare."

"Wrong with what?"

"Australia."

In Liebermann's window, a clutter of objects below the bechained brass lamps, the Tiffany nonsense. Trays of rings and necklaces. Porcelain. A tall, flashy chess set, the black men red. A horse-pistol. A glass case with a stuffed brown bird in it. An eighteenth-centuryish painting of a man in a wig looking at some dog-like sheep. Silver.

"Look at these jade things," said Susan.

Discs of green jade carved and pierced, flowers, curled dragons.

"How would you like that bird?" said David.

"Let's go in and look round," said Susan.

"You could say, 'Oh, that? That's my stuffed bird.'"

From the end of the long red strip of carpet, Mr. Liebermann looked at them over his glasses but did not get up. David was drawn past Samurai armour, marble busts of Bach and Beethoven, an elephant's foot bristling with swords and walking-sticks, to a square glass case containing a stuffed squirrel.

Strips of gilt beading ran round the base of the squirrel's black lacquered case – tarnished, crackled gilt but splendid – a surviving, a reminder . . . It had not all been floral horror and overstuffed arm-chairs.

The bird's case, on the other hand, was domed and suggested the worst of wax lilies and cemeteries and the Albert Memorial.

He studied the squirrel; even its eyes were dusty. It was faded, mangy, moth-eaten, wired to its branch at a drunken angle. Yet the squirrel, he decided, was more attractive than the bird. It was difficult to relate to birds.

And for another thing, the papier-mâché flora of the squirrel's background was of distinctly superior workmanship.

Description:

Squirrel Falling Off a Branch
(*Gift of D. Appleby Esq.*)

Or the authority of Latin?

Nutty Nuttimus

"Was there something?" said Mr. Liebermann.

"What were these jade things for?" said Susan.

Or simplicity?

A Squirrel

It was strange that one never met those kinds of people. Or met anyone who *had* met them. The people who made wax lilies, or papier-mâché flora, or plastic swords and pistols for antique bars, or giant bottles, or poker-work mottoes, or sang *scoobie-doobie* for a living behind pop stars. At a party, in a bar, what could one reply?

Well, I'm in the plastic dogturd business.

Oh. . . .

"A lovely piece. They used to sew them on their clothes," said Mr. Liebermann.

"Look, David!"

She held out the jade disc on her palm. Its green was mysterious, grey in some lights, colour changing with the shadows of her fingers underneath it. She turned the soft, cool stone admiring the intricacy of the carving, the dragon's convolutions.

"Some ladies wear them as pendants," said Mr. Liebermann.

"Do you like it?" said David.

"Touch it," she said.

"Two hundred years old. More," said Mr. Liebermann.

"How much is it?" said David.

"It's ridiculous," said Mr. Liebermann. "I don't know why I do it. Forty dollars."

"We'll take it."

"No, David! That's far too much."

"With a chain."

Mr. Liebermann took a length of tarnished chain from a big cardboard box of oddments and ran it through a handful of damp wadding. The shop smelled suddenly of lemons.

"A nice little box?"

"Put it on," said David. "Wear it."

"Can you do the clasp?" she said.

"Ten for the squirrel," said David, looking up.

After the close warmth of the shop, the raw wind funnelling down the street from the mountain seemed to cut more bitterly than before.

"Jesus Christ!" exclaimed David, rigid as the wind hit him. "I must be stark bonkers! England'll be knee-deep in bloody daffodils by now."

The downtown streets and pavements were clear and dry but in the suburbs out towards *Merrymount,* down side streets, in gardens and the corners of parking lots the blackened banks of rotting snow lingered on and on.

Susan turned her back to the wind and held the top of her coat open.

"Beautiful," she said.

"They certainly are," said David.

"You know what I like? I like to think of the people who wore this before. And now I'm wearing it."

"Garry was telling me a thing about that," he said. "That he'd heard in Vancouver."

"Westlake?"

"Umm. He said that very old Chinese men there get together in a darkened room over a grocery store and drink tea and feel pieces of jade under water."

"That's beautiful," said Susan. "Like the cherry blossom."

"Right. And it's beautiful," said David, "because . . ."

"Because they're going to die," said Susan.

David set his squirrel down on the pavement. He pulled Susan against him and kissed her.

"That's why I love you," he said. "Because you understand that. Really, really understand."

"And I love you because you know things like that to tell me."

"Why else?"

"Because you're beautiful," she said.

"That's very true," he said, bending to pick up the squirrel. Overbalancing, scooping the case, he staggered into a juggling run for five or six yards. Then he stood facing her clutching the glass case safe against his chest, laughing.

"You're drunken," she said.

"Hey, I've just thought of something. Won't your parents ask you where you got the jade thing?"

"I'll tell them I got it in Chinatown or something. They wouldn't know the difference."

"How *goes* the Home Front?"

"Same. She's crazy. Tonight she said, 'I suppose you're going out with that man, little whore,' and then as I was going out the door she said, 'Enjoy yourself while you're young, dear.'"

"Unsettling," said David.

"And my dad calls you The Teacher and *shaykh* – The Old Man."

"That's not nice."

"Oh, and when he came in tonight and they were having supper he was tearing a loaf of bread in half and . . ."

"*Tearing?*"

"It's Syrian bread – flat sort of like a pancake but bread."

"Oh."

"And he said, 'Look, missy! This going to happen to the *shaykh*.'"

"Charming!"

"'When the muscle finished with him,' and he dropped the piece of bread on the floor and stamped on it."

"Well, that's not very nice," said David. "What's 'the muscle'?"

"Oh, he says he's hired two guys to beat you up with baseball bats. Cost him a hundred and fifty."

David laughed.

"And where would one hire such desperadoes?"

"You're really weird," said Susan. "You're so British, you know that?"

"Why?"

"Because it happens every day, that's why. For debts and gambling. Don't you read the papers?"

"And you mean – you really think he *has*?"

"No. It's all talk."

"Hey, wait a minute. If he *has*, that means he knows who I am."

She shrugged.

"I mean, if they *know*," said David, "why don't they *do* something? Phone the school, the Board."

"They're crazy."

"Yes, but . . ."

"They don't know," said Susan. "But even if they do, they wouldn't really know what to do about it. They're not educated people."

"Well, I don't know," said David. "It just doesn't make sense to me."

They turned up Stanley Street towards *The Delta*. The squirrel was getting heavy. Who had told her mother in the first place? And why not his name? Incomprehensible. His left hand and forearm felt numb, pins and needles. Was it merely the awkwardness and weight of the glass case? Or was it a message from the DEW line? He imagined his heart. He would, in future, drink less.

Warm light poured out onto the pavement from the *Pam-Pam*. They could smell coffee.

"I've been banned from there," said Susan.

David shifted the case and worked his hand.

"Well, I don't know," he said. "I just don't understand what's going on."

The Delta was divided into two sections. The front sold paperbacks, records and artistic oddments; the back room, under the same management, was a folksong centre. There was half an hour to wait before the first set.

Susan had wandered off and was flipping through a tray of records. David stood facing one of the book racks. The fluorescent light seemed extraordinarily bright; it also seemed to be humming. He stared mesmerised at the shiny books. He felt as if he was enclosed in a transparent envelope, remote from the sounds about him yet sudden words and sentences rang strange and clear. He had to concentrate to read the words on pages for the line kept slipping into a blur of black on white, designs, grey abstractions. He found himself accompanying the light fixture in a monotone hum. He did not want to move; he just wanted to stand where he was, staring at the shiny covers and doing his hum. It had become important to him not to let the hum falter or fail. Yet he also felt anxious, anxious that people would stare at him, think him drunk, challenge him, demand things of him.

Two girls with lots of thigh were leaning on the counter talking to the bearded man, the manager. The bearded man said,

"In the mountains we were free."

Most of the books in the section in front of him seemed to have been printed in California and had introductions by Doctors of Philosophy from Berkeley.

. . . this searing document . . .

He moved the squirrel along with his foot.

. . . little-known aspects of Victorian . . .

. . . a compassionate exploration of the copraphiliac's world . . .

Would it not be passing brave to be a Doctor of Philosophy? And ride in triumph through Persepolis?

At the end of the book rack was a stand of things on thongs and hairy ties. The labels said,

handwoven by Michael

A record-player suddenly produced Joan Baez.

"Arnold! Where's the *Nescafé?*"

He looked round for Susan. She was bending over a table which displayed a lot of misshapen Eskimo carvings; lumpy owls, ducks with glued necks and beaks, walruses with missing tusks, lobotomized-looking seals.

"No," said the bearded man, "I always add wheat-germ."

It was sinister, really. Eskimo carvings were on sale in department stores, airports, boutiques, craft shops, galleries and gift stores from Glace Bay to Vancouver. Had ever such a tiny people produced so many artists, so many artifacts?

NO. Such a tiny people never had.

Nobody was really fooled.

Herds of Eskimo rounded up by the bully-boys of the Eaton-Simpson-Morgan Combine. Into the compounds. Disciplining under Major Grigson. Distribution of soap-stone, and the pictorial *How to Carve With Your Black and Decker* booklets.

"Have you got the blue tickets, Arnold!"

He was aware of movement, people; the shop was filling up. One of the girls at the counter had a hole the size of a dime in her black tights through which a lump of white leg protruded. It looked like a disease.

More books. Many copies of *Black Like Me*. Astrology ca-ca. Diabolism ca-ca. Occult ca-ca. Zen ca-ca.

Guitar Manuals:

> *Sing Out With Pete Seeger*
> *Bluegrass for Beginners*
> *Woodie Guthrie Simplified*

Somebody bumped into him. He swayed and turned.

The woman – Mrs. Bearded? – a lank-haired slattern wearing a black turtleneck and a handcrafted skirt, was setting up a baize-covered cardtable at the entrance to the back room.

"Thank Christ," said David. "My legs ache."

They joined the line beside the tray of $1.39 Bargain Records.

"I hope he's good," said Susan.

> *Latvian Ensemble*
> *Folkloric Favourites*

"That bearded man's called Arnold," said David.

> *Songs the Wobblies Sang*
> *The World's Greatest Cantor*

For two dollars, the woman tore off a blue cloakroom ticket and sloshed hot water into a cup of *Nescafé*, stirring it with a plastic spoon. On the top of each cup whirled a brown lump of undissolved coffee. Another plastic spoon was stuck in an open five-pound box of sugar. Under the guise of adding sugar and stirring, David captured his lump and buried it in the sugar-box.

Sitting down in the semi-gloom at a table covered with a red and white checkered cloth and a candle in a bowl-thing covered with nylon netting was nicer. He tucked his squirrel under his chair. He had ignored the ill-bred stares and comments. Sipping the coffee, he looked round at the faithful; most of them were kids but there were a few older people. Four tables away was the black shape of a man with a monstrous hunchback.

David began to feel stronger; the coffee was doing him good. Susan was picking at the candle, feeding it dribbles of wax. The chairs, though a welcome relief from standing, were authentically uncomfortable. He had haunted jazz and blues clubs since the age of fifteen; the chairs were always uncomfortable whether the club was in England, France, Germany, or Canada. Non-commercial chairs, chairs untainted by materialism, pure chairs, *folk* chairs.

Under the spotlight on the tiny stage, a stool and a large black guitar-case waited.

David looked away, staring into the candle-flame which climbed and flared as Susan fed it wax. He giggled. *Woodie Guthrie Simplified.* A difficult feat. The room was filling quickly. Sentences, phrases kept coming to him out of the heat and babble. People pushing past against his chair. The hunchback got to his feet, calling, "Marcie! Over here, Marcie!" As the hunchback moved into the soupy yellow light of one of the spots, David saw that he wasn't a hunchback at all. He was wearing a long bongo drum. And stranger still, he was wearing checked Bermuda shorts with a matching jacket.

Bearded Arnold, to much applause, made his way to the tiny stage and raised the microphone.

"Ladies and Gentlemen! Tonight it's my pleasure to introduce to you and to the Montreal folk-scene one of the Grand Old Men of the blues. I'm proud to present one of the truly great bluesmen – Blind Foxy John!"

Arnold fumbled in the curtains and led the old man out. During the applause, Blind Foxy John felt for the edge of the stool and sat down. His fingers searched out for the microphone. He was wearing a blue serge suit, white shirt, a black string-tie. His black work boots gleamed. The light flashed on his dark glasses.

His fingers found the catches of the guitar-case and lifted out a battered old *Steel National*. He ran a yellow duster over the neck and then played a few notes, tuning.

Into the silence, he began to play chords, plaintive runs which descended into the continuing base. He raised his head and spoke over the music.

"Some people say that the blues is a cow wanta see her calf, but I don't say it like that. I say it's a man that's got a companion, and she turn him down, and things like that happens, you know – and tha's where I gets the blues – when I wanta see my baby and wanta see her bad – "

Blues figures accompanied and punctuated the flow of his voice. Some words half-lifted into song.

". . . . . . well, I tell you, it really worries me just to think, I used to have a sweet little girl – you know, name *Es*telle. An' we used to go to school together, an' we nach'ly grew up together, you know, grew up together . . . in other words, I wanted to love her . . . and axed her mother for her . . . and whereat she turned me down – and that cause me to sing the blues. They turned me down, and then I just got to sitting down thinking, you understand, and then I thought of a song, and I started to drinking . . . the blues the only thing that gives me consolation.

A blind man he seen her,
A dumb man called her name!
Little *Es*telle. Down in Arkansas. Goatshead, Arkansas."

The old man chuckled and mumbled something. A long descending blues run ending in a chord.

"We coloured people have had so much trouble, we's the one nation is, we try to be happy anyway – you ever noticed that? – it's because we have never had so much, you understand. . . . And I remember we cleaned up a whole bottom, you know, bottom with willows. Willows was thick and I stalled four mules to a wagon, you understand, four mules, you know, out in the bottom cleaning it up.

We had to clean it up in the winter so that we could work it that summer. . . ."

Something began to circle in David's mind, nagging, worrying, a feeling of recognition.

"The thing I think about the blues *is* – it didn't happen in the North – in Chicago, New York, Philadelphia, Pennsylvania, wha'soever it is – it didn't start in the East – neither in the West – it started in the South, from what I'm thinkin'.

Where the Yazoo cross the Yellow Dog. . . ."

The old man nodded.

"Yeah, all the nigra want to go to the North. Travel on, you know. Travel on down the line."

"Yeah!" said the young man with the bongo drum. "Travel on down that line."

His voice climbing, the old man sang,

Michigan water taste like sherry-wine,
Mississippi water taste like turpentine . . .

He chuckled, nodding again.

"Taste like turpentine," he repeated.

"And that's a bitter taste, man!" said the bongo boy.

David felt puzzled. The song was one of Jelly Roll Morton's. Recorded by Lomax for the Library of Congress – a series recorded not long before Morton's death. The old man's voice had even climbed towards Morton's thin, whimsical tone. Perhaps he had known him, heard him sing?

"We really want to know why, and how come a man have the blues. I worked on levee camps, extra gangs, road camps and rock camps, cotton, worked near every place, and I hear guys singin' *un-hmm* this and *mmmmmmm* that, and I want to know and I want to get to think plainly that the blues is something that's from the heart – I know *that* and it expressing his feeling about *how* he felt to the people. I've known guys that wanted to cuss out the boss and he was afraid to go up to his face and tell him what he wanted to tell him, and I've heard them sing those things – sing words, you know, – back to the boss – just behind the wagon, hookin' up to the horses or somethin' or 'nuther – or the mules or something, and then he'd go to work and go to singing and say things to the horse, you know, horse, make like the mule stepped on his foot – say 'Get off my foot, goddam it!' or something like that, and he meant he was talking to the boss. 'You son of a bitch, you' say 'you got no business on my—, stay off my foot' and such things as that. . . ."

"Way to go!" said the bongo man.

"Yeah, man," said another voice.

"Beautiful, beautiful," said a girl's voice.

Lifting his head, Blind Foxy John sang unaccompanied,

Blind Foxy John done gone
Blind Foxy John done gone
He's from the County Farm
They didn't know his name
They didn't know his name
He had a long chain on . . .

The song was not American; its cadences went back to the beginnings of slavery, to a past that conjured Africa. At the end of each line, David heard the rows of picks falling on stone, the *thunk* of the biting axes, the grunts of the chained convicts as they swung to the leader's chant.

The nag of recognition drew to certainty. He knew where he had heard Blind Foxy John's stories before. On a record. And Blind Foxy John hadn't been telling them; those men were long dead.

He remembered devouring what books there were then, when he was fourteen and fifteen, remembered the badly printed bulletins and discographies from all the fanatical jazz societies, the prized records pirated from America, the endless evenings and weekends listening to the music America ignored. It was one of Tony's records, one his uncle had brought back from New York. A Lomax record. A field-recording made in the forties of old lifers in a southern pen.

"The bloody old fraud!" said David. "He's getting all this stuff from records."

"*Shss!*" said a voice.

"What do you mean?" said Susan.

"You'll see," said David. "He'll tell a story about a man called Mr.

72

White who gave all the animals born black to the Negroes. I know this stuff. I remember now."

"*Shss!*" said voices.

"Shss, yourself!" said David.

The blues run ended in a chord.

"And I've known, uh, it was a nigra and a white standin' well, it was right at railroad crossing, you know, just as you get in town like where you cross the railroad tracks? The white man was telling the nigra what he wanted him to do – and it was a nigra was comin' driving a wagon with a grey mule and a black mule to the wagon, see. So this nigra drove up to the crossing..."

"He's going to have to call the grey mule 'Mister'," said David.

"... the mules was tryin' to pull over and he kept saying 'Get up, giddup.' The white man holler up there, ask him, 'Hey,' says, 'Do you know that's a white mule you talkin' to?' He says, 'Oh yes, sir! Giddup, Mister Mule!'"

Through the laughter, David said, "This is disgraceful!"

"How did you know?" said Susan.

"It's a record for Christ's sake! I told you."

"And I'm minded they was a kind of tobacco called *Prince Albert Tobacco*. That were all down through Arkansas, down Goulds, Dumas, Yonquipin ... and you didn't say, 'Gimme a can of *Prince Albert*.' You know that? You know what you say?"

"Yes," called David. "I *do* know. You said, 'Gimme a can of MISTER *Prince Albert*' because he was a white man. And I know because I heard it on the same record you did and you ought to be ashamed of yourself!"

Keep quiet!

"What the brother say?" said Blind Foxy John.

"You're a bloody fraud!" shouted David.

Throw him out!

Shame!

"David! Come on! We'd better go."

"He's getting it all from a record!"

The uproar rose. The lights were turned up.

He's drunk! Get him out!

73

Turning in the direction of the voice, David shouted, "I am *not drunk*! It's a 1947 Alan Lomax record!"

"PLEASE," bellowed Bearded Arnold from the doorway. "PLEASE."

"Come on, David!"

He pushed back his chair and stood up.

"You don't insult a man that's worked in the cotton!" yelled Bongo, also getting to his feet.

"Shut-up, Pimples!" called Susan.

"The nearest he's been to cotton," yelled David, "is his undershirt!"

"PLEASE!" yelled Arnold.

"You'd better better blow, man," said Bongo.

"What happened to your trousers?" said David.

"We don't need racists here," said Bongo.

"You're lucky you're wearing a drum," said David.

His upper arm was grasped; glass shattered as he turned; he found his face inches from that of Bearded Arnold.

"My squirrel's broken," said David.

"You'll feel better," said Arnold, "in the fresh air."

A few late night window-shoppers. Couples. University students in lettered jackets. It was not as cold as it had been earlier because the gusting winds had dropped. David felt immensely tired and could not keep from yawning as they walked along. His legs felt leaden. Susan's leather coat creaked. The taste of the root beer lingered; he thought it one of the most truly disgusting things he'd ever tasted. And made from the root of *what* was beyond his imagination. They turned off Ste. Catherine up Mansfield and stopped to peer into the windows of Mr. Heinemann's bookshop.

"I wouldn't mind that," said David, pointing to a facsimile of the Quarto *Hamlet*.

"I'd rather have a paperback," said Susan.

Within the curve of McGill University gates, they stopped to light cigarettes and then propped themselves against the low wall watching the procession of cars along Sherbrooke, the yellow beacons of taxis gliding towards them along the night. Susan pulled up the deep collar of her coat.

"You look like a spy. A beautiful spy," said David.

A couple walked past.

"What's the matter?"

"Nothing," she said. "Why?"

"You don't seem to be saying much."

She shrugged.

A bus roared past dragging coldness after it.

She stood up and pulled down the skirts of her coat. Looking about on the pavement near David's feet, she said, "Where's the squirrel?"

Back in the A&W sitting on the counter. Staring up with its dusty little eyes at the sign which said:

The Hamburgers That AM Burgers.

"No, let's leave it there," he said.

The picture grew elegiac in his mind. The plastic orange bobbing on the surface of the tank of orange liquid. The plastic-topped mushroom stools. Fluorescent acres of white plastic table-tops. The sticky, squidgy containers of ketchup and mustard. And on the clean and gleaming counter, the squirrel sitting like a reproach.

Susan flicked her cigarette-end across the pavement onto the road where it showered sparks. The wind of a passing car trundled it out towards the crown of the road.

"Are you going to make application here?" he said.

"McGill? Hadn't thought about it."

"You'd better start doing some work soon, you know. It's not long now to the matrics."

"I suppose it isn't," she said.

"It's Easter holidays next week and then there'll be about two weeks in April and then the whole of May. And exams start on the second of June. Or the fourth, maybe. So that's only seven or eight weeks."

"Yes," she said.

"Think you'll pass?"

"I don't know."

"Well, don't you think . . ."

"O.K. There's seven or eight weeks. O.K. Don't start on about it again."

"I'm not 'starting on' but it's pretty important."

"It might be important to *you*."

"What's *that* supposed to mean?"

She shrugged and pushed her hands deep into her pockets.

"What's it *matter*!" she said. "I expect I'll be dead by the time I'm twenty-one or so anyway."

"What do you mean by *that*?"

"I just feel I will be, that's all."

"But why should you be? You haven't got a disease or something, have you?"

"It's just something I feel."

"Well that doesn't make much sense."

"I'm sorry my feelings don't make sense to you."

"Oh, for Christ's sake!"

He looked at her profile as she studied the roof of the Three-Minute-Carwash opposite.

"Susan?"

"What?"

"What are we quarreling about?"

"I don't know. I'm sorry. I just don't like being pushed."

They were silent.

"But don't you think university'd be interesting?"

"No."

"But why? I'm not trying to push. I just want to know. O.K.? I mean, you read a lot anyway. You like books."

"If I was doing just the things I liked the way you did in England maybe I would like it. I don't know. But it isn't like that here. I'm not interested in science and sociology and French and I don't want to sit in classes of three hundred doing crap like Freshman Composition."

"Well, you wouldn't have to put up with it for long, would you?"

"I don't want to put up with it at all."

A group of people walked past talking loudly. One of the men stared at them.

"O.K.," said David, when they had passed. "Here's the lowest common denominator, then. You need the bit of paper you get at the end. What sort of job can you get without a degree?"

"All sorts of jobs."

"Like what?"

"I don't *give* a shit. I'd *rather* be a secretary or work in Eaton's. I'd exchange a piece of my time for money – and that's all. And then they can't touch me."

"Oh, yes!" said David. "Oh, yes, I can just see it. Especially you. Have you ever worked in a factory? Or behind a counter? Or in a restaurant?"

"No."

"Well, *I* have. And I don't think you'd like it. You're just being romantic."

"Maybe. I don't *expect* to like it. And if being 'realistic' means like most people I'd *rather* be romantic."

"Look, Susan. I'm really not trying to quarrel. Honestly. I just want to know how you feel, that's all. I mean, a minute ago you said 'They can't touch me.' What did you mean by that?"

"I meant that I know who I am. I don't want to go to university or have a 'career' because it makes you into a different kind of person."

"How?"

"Well think of English. That's all that interests me, anyway. Literature's about feelings. And reading a lot of boring old crap kills that. It changes you."

"Now just wait . . ."

"Look, I was born on Drolet in the east end, right? And I'm not going to let anyone turn me into a nice middle-class McGill girl who knows all about Shakespeare's fucking will or some bunch of horseshit."

"I don't think it need mean that," said David.

"Well you don't think very much then, do you?"

David sighed.

"And don't sigh at *me*."

"Well," said David, "it's your life."

"You're damn right it is!" she said.

David shook his head.

"Look at what comes out the other end," she said. "If it meant anything to them, would they be the kind of people they are? Would they kiss ass to work for *Sun Life* and *IBM* and go into teaching?"

"Well, you can't . . ."

"I'm not cashing in *my* feelings for a piece of paper!" she said.

"What about me?" said David, turning to her. *"I've* been to a university and *I* teach."

"Well, I think it's different in England somehow – and you're you – you're special."

"Thank you kindly," he said, bobbing a curtsy.

"I'm trying to talk to you, David. Stop fooling around. I don't feel like it."

"O.K.," he said "But you can't expect *not* to change, can you?"

"No, of course not. But I'm going to become more me. I'm not going to have me changed to fit in with them."

"Well . . . I don't know . . . I mean, are people *really* that much changed by going to university or doing an interesting job? Distorted by it?"

Susan turned round and stared through the railings across the lawns towards the library. Three windows on the top floor were lighted. She started to scrape a pencil-stub on the rough stone of the wall.

"My sister," she said. "She used to be an O.K. person. I really used to like her. But it's all changed now."

"How do you mean?"

"She used to read a lot – give me books. She used to see all the movies. We used to go to the *Tête de l'Art* and the *Showbar* and the *Casa Loma* and she used to go to New York on weekends to hear Miles and Monk at the *Vanguard* – she really used to *care*. And she was going around with a poet – well, he used to write anyway. And at home she always stood up for me when they started. But now she's working, she's different. Since she quit school. Two years and she's a different person. She's always having her hair done and ironing blouses and Mr. Courteney said this, Mr. Courteney said that, the girls were saying, I went on an errand to Mr. Courteney's house. . . . Shit!"

"Well not wearing jeans to work or something isn't . . ."

"It's that job at COXM. Since she's been there . . . she stayed up all one night at home writing *Dentaflor* on balloons with a magic marker because the printer had let them down and as a reward they let her go up in the COXM helicopter and release them over Fairview Shopping Centre. How about that!"

"O.K. but . . ."

"No! She was *thrilled*. Don't you understand? And now it's always, 'Yes, Susan. Don't sit like that.' As if she hadn't *seen* a crotch before. 'Really, Susan! Don't be vulgar.' And this is the strangest – really *weird* – she pretends she doesn't screw anymore. Oh, Jesus – and the guy she's going around with! A real prick. A guy about forty with a pot-belly – an industrial fucking chemicals salesman."

She threw the pencil-stub over the railings and turned round to stare at him.

"Why?" she said. "How can you have liked Coltrane and Miles and Sonny Rollins and become like *that*?"

David shrugged.

"I don't know," he said.

"Got a cigarette?" she said.

The matches kept wavering out.

"I'm freezing," she said.

"That is, of course," he said, "arguing from only one case."

"Oh, *bullshit*!" she said. "Bullshit! You're always trying to avoid the point with *words*!"

They were silent. David smoked intently.

"You always say you want to write – " he said at length. "You've got to study other writers to do that."

"There's libraries and bookshops."

"And nobody can help you?"

"Not in there," she said, turning to look through the railings again.

"Well, whatever you say, I think you need some kind of perspective. A sort of – I don't know – I don't want to sound pompous – but a sense of the – *tradition*."

"I'll buy a *Penguin*," she said.

"I think you're making a big mistake."

She shrugged.

"If I am, I can go to nightschool, can't I?" she said. "Or the Pig Farm or something."

"The *what?*"

"Macdonald College."

"Oh. I suppose so."

"I'd better go," she said. "We're not enjoying ourselves any more."

"No, don't go. Don't be silly. We're only discussing something."

"No, we're not," she said.

She walked over to the curb and waved down an approaching cab.

"We're not enjoying ourselves and we're not discussing anything, David," she said as she got into the back seat. "You shouldn't lie to yourself."

As he closed the door, something perverse made him say, "Remember. There's only eight weeks."

One foot on the deserted pavement, one foot in the gutter, David limped rhythmically westward. It seemed to fit his mood.

He had watched the taxi until its tail-lights had merged into traffic, hoping that she might wave, turn to look at him.

Susan.

Quite, quite wrong, of course. Wilful. Moody. Perhaps her period was approaching. He felt quite sober, the drinks faded leaving him withdrawn, sodden with fatigue. Hot grit behind the eyes.

Yes, a sense of the *tradition*. She would discover the need for discipline – that necessary humility in the face of those who were truly great. He found himself staring down the vistas of English Literature at all the monuments of unaging intellect which had constituted his education. The Battle of Malden, The Vision of Caedmon, The Dream of the Rood, The Nightmare of Nignog, Cynewulf and the Three Little Pigs, Gammer Gurton's Grotty Needle.

Yes, that was it! Alliteration!
Swooning Swinburne
Tedious Tennyson
Past the Van Horne house with its graceful conservatory. All threatened with demolition. Barbarism not unexpected from people blunted by hamburger and ravaged by root beer.
Balls-Aching Addison
Suckholing Steele
Past the Ritz Carlton, black and gold, splendidly English.
SHITTY *"Spectator"*
The Dominion Gallery
    (All Paintings! European Artists!
    Regular $300 Now Only $125.
    Including Frame!)
Jumbo Johnson
Brown-nose Boswell
Approaching his favourite Montreal shop, limping down the three shallow steps to its lighted window.
The Petit Musée.

It was while he was gazing into the window at the objects – Persian miniatures, Pre-Columbian figurines, flintlocks, Bambara carvings, armour, coins, a tiny faience ushabti, a Ming vase, a necklace from an Egyptian tomb, a Dogon ancestor figure – gazing and trying to realize some drifting, unformed, disturbing comparison between the display and his university education that he first became aware of the man.

The man must have been behind him for some time. Now he was seeming to study the window display in *Holt Renfrew*. A tall man. A black overcoat. Surely not on *Sherbrooke*!

Slowly, David mounted the steps to pavement level, casually turned and drifted two stores down where he stopped to stare unseeingly at a display of Sheffield Plate. The man strolled closer and stopped to look in the window of the *Petit Musée – but without going down the steps*. Six foot three, at least. A black hat. Gloves.

Could they get prints from human flesh?

He walked away fast to the corner of Guy and turned down past the bank and the Medical Arts building. He looked back. The man was standing on the corner. David crossed through the traffic and reached the other side. The lights changed. The man was crossing, turning down, not hurrying.

How was it going to be? Under a car, a bus? He glanced back. Home wasn't the answer. Perhaps – there was a faint chance – they still didn't know where he lived. And two flights of stairs with burned-out lights would be giving the bastard a gift. Gagnon wouldn't be any help – *he'd* probably join in. Was it her father? Or a Muscle?

Music.

La Source on the corner of Lincoln. David leaped up the steps and in through the heavy wooden door. He got a place at the bar commanding the doorway.

Under no circumstances bolt for the washroom.

"Oh, Scotch. Ice. Water."

He found that he felt sick. His heart was thumping in his throat. Heart-attack symptoms in his left arm. He looked at his watch. One a.m. He could phone Jim to come and get him. If Jim was in. But he'd probably be with Lise. He rattled the plastic spear around in the ice-cubes. He tried the point of the spear against the bar. No help there. He got up and went to the door and looked out. The man was nowhere in sight. But sitting in a parked car, lurking in a doorway? He'd have a cold lurk because David decided that he'd wait until the bar closed – and then, down Guy to Ste. Catherine. Lights. People. And a cab from there. *A cab!* Of course! Why hadn't he thought of that? He could phone one from the bar.

As he climbed onto his stool again he accidentally nudged the man beside him.

"I'm terribly sorry," said David.

The man mopped up the spots of drink with a cardboard coaster. A small man wearing a dark suit, a pullover, a tie with a tiny knot. A nasty Follet-like moustache.

"What part of England are you from?" said the man.

"London," said David promptly.

Untrue, but it was the only English place most Canadians had heard of. If he said Southbourne, *they* always said, "That's near London, isn't it?"

"I could tell your accent right away," said the man.

"This is only my second year here," said David.

"A bit colder than England, eh?" said the man.

"It certainly is," said David.

"And hotter in the summer," said the man.

"It sure is," said David, an Americanism of which he was quite proud.

The sick feeling was going away. He emptied a pottery canoe of peanuts and sipped the scotch.

"Yes," said the man. "I'm very interested in England. And Peru."

"Oh?" said David.

"Yes, Stonehenge. It's one of my special interests, Stonehenge. Have you been there?"

"Yes. I've been a few times. It's very impressive."

"You could say that Stonehenge formed the *centre* of my special interests."

He looked at David intently and then said, "Would you like another of those? Scotch? Yes, an amazing structure."

How nice! Sitting talking to this nice small man. Perhaps later he'd like to share a cab? And if not, down the seven steps together and across the pavement to the safety of the cab door. *I've much enjoyed* . . . Muscle, if he was there, impotent.

"Are you interested in the Druids?" asked David.

"Druids!" The man laughed. "No, no, no. Not Druids."

He put his hand on David's arm.

"What interests me is the extra-terrestrial aspects."

"Oh," said David.

He started on a wicker basket of pretzels.

"Yes," said the man. "Take England. Just talking about England now. Stonehenge. The celebrated Uffington White Horse. Glastonbury earthworks. The Long Man of Wiltshire. Eh?"

"Yes?"

"Ever hear of the Nazca Lines in Peru? No, eh? *You can't see them from the ground!*"

"Really?" said David.

"But from a plane – from a plane they stretch for miles – patterns, diagrams. Now what does that suggest?"

"I don't know," said David.

"Some so-called scholars have suggested that we're dealing with irrigation ditches," said the man. "Irrigation ditches. In the shape of an accurate map of the heavens!"

"Well, that's something I've never . . ."

"And you can't see them from the ground."

David looked away from the man's eyes, and staring down into the pretzel-basket, shook his head.

"In all these things, you see," said the man, "the thing to keep in mind is *viewed from a height.*"

David nodded slowly. He could feel his face beginning to ache into a rictus of attention.

"Now let me ask you a question. Why do so many straight lines *converge* on Stonehenge?"

David grimaced to indicate ignorance.

"Why were the famous blue stones brought all the way to Stonehenge from the Prescelly Hills in Wales?"

David did another face.

"Could they have been *power-centres*?" said the man.

"Power-centres?"

"Re-fuelling points."

"Re-fuelling?"

"Galactic vehicles," said the man.

"Flying . . . . . ?"

"*Saucers.* Exactly. Exactly. You see?" said the man.

"Well, I'd never thought of that," said David.

"Had you ever thought," said the man, "that they acted as a kind of condenser for building up electromagnetic power in the same way that piezoelectricity does in twenty different classes of crystal structures?"

"No," said David.

Chapter Five

Jim had marked all his Easter exam papers on the first day of the holiday; David had left his to the last. He had set his alarm and got up at six; he had even gone out after breakfast and bought an expensive red ballpoint. In two hours he had marked thirteen papers; roughly one hundred and forty to go.

He slashed through a few run-on sentences, spelling mistakes, and peculiarities of punctuation and then relapsed into staring out of the window.

It was nice enough to go out for a walk. Without an overcoat.

When they burn all the lovely golden leaves on my street in the Fall I always cry.

LIAR he printed in the margin.

Listlessly through the next, the pile heavy on his knee. A lad who had watched a documentary on CBC about lighthouses and found it "very illuminating."

Oh, God!

The Greatness of Modern Popular Music of Today.

Mayor Drapeau – Our Little Dynamo.

"Oh, fucking hell!" sighed David.

Leap screaming from the window waving genitals and manuscript.

Plattsburg – My Utopia.

"Fuck this for a lark!" said David. "I can't take much more."

Jim grunted; he was reading the *Gazette*.

David began to click the button on his pen to the tune of "Hitler Has Only Got One Ball"; pains in his chest; breathing was becoming difficult. Beside his chair sat four more fucking great bulging envelopes full.

Was his throat becoming sore?

Oh, for a whole class – all his classes – to do what Susan had done! The saving in time and energy! In boredom. *His* classes, of course, had written pages:

"The poet uses words well. There is a good use of rhythm and rhyme (eg. 'red' and 'head') and subtle use of imagery, figures of speech and smilies. The poet says what he had to say well with vivid colour words."

Howie Bunceford, Susan's English teacher and Head of the English Department, had been very cross when he had shown her literature paper around the Men's Staffroom on the last day.

"That girl," Bunceford had declared, "is too big for her boots."

Ignorant.

Lack of RESPECT.

"She'll get her come-uppance in the Matrics," Bunceford had said.

Give her zero.

He could only remember the first four lines of the sight poem which Bunceford had set for all the grade eleven classes – he *must* learn the rest.

Been in trouble before, that girl.

Like Frances Campbell. There's another.

But what ripe lines they were:

What is there other than colour and light?

Spring has the brush – let her paint.

Splashing the atmosphere azure and red:

Out of the way! it will drip on your head!

In response to the poem, Susan had written,

"I don't want to waste my time writing about bad poetry."

Strange that Bunceford had been so cross. Unlike him. Unless *he* had perpetrated the poem?

David had very little contact with Bunceford, for Howie, as he was called, spent the greater part of his time in the book stockroom implementing the Board's Condition Evaluation System, counting the sets of *Moonfleet* and *Cue for Treason*, poring over *Ancient Myths Retold for Modern Youth*, deliberating over grubby copies of *On the Edge of the Something Forest or Jungle* by creepy Albert Schweitzer.

The Board's Condition Evaluation System required all texts to be categorized as:

Good Condition
Fair Condition
To Be Replaced Within Two Years
To Be Replaced.

Such agonies of decision occupied Howie three periods per day. He was frequently to be seen standing motionless in the bookroom as though paralysed by his responsibility.

He issued sporadic purple bulletins and exhortations to the Department on the subject of ink-stains, obscene illustration of the text, defacement in general, and loose spines. Most of his other communications concerned the organization of the school-wide essay contest during National Fire Prevention Week and the logistics of the annual "What *I* Can Do To Help The Red Cross."

Apart from such professional concerns, Howie's conversation was limited to the subject of his cottage on Lake Memphramagog. He was always closing the cottage, opening the cottage, repairing the cottage, putting screens on the cottage, taking them off, repointing the cottage's fieldstone barbeque-pit, painting, sheathing or insulating the cottage.

Against weeds and other undesirable flora, he pursued a scorched-earth policy; he harried unmercifully the local skunks, squirrels, and racoons; he waged war against the blackfly, the mosquito, and the fieldmouse.

Howie was flabby and extraordinarily pink. He kept a tablet of soap and a face-cloth in his locker. His handshake was flaccid. It was claimed by a group of grade eleven students to whom he taught Latin that he traditionally turned over two pages in Caesar to avoid a photo of a naked statue, thus causing a shipload of mariners on page thirteen to be strengthening the walls of the city against their approach on page sixteen. He never used the urinal while anyone else was there. He was so mild, affable and avuncular, so *benign*, as to seem without opinion. When he sat down he seemed to spread. He always reminded David of the expression "a sack of loose shit."

But, as evidenced in his poetry, there was a sterner and more anguished side to Howie's nature. His poems had been published in the *Montreal Star*, local Quebec papers, the *PAPT Teachers Magazine*, and had twice won the Jackpot on COXM's *Pinkerton's Posy Contest*.

Susan said that he often read work-in-progress to his grade eleven classes, offering insights such as only he could give into technical aspects of composition. He was, apparently, gathering a body of work to be published under the title *Impulse From A Vernal Wood*.

David delighted in each new addition to the canon and kept a file of clippings. He knew some poems by heart and recited them when drunk. His favourites were entitled *Dear Old Days* and *The Mountain and the Cottage – A Sonnet*.

Dear Old Days had first appeared in the school newspaper, *The Merrymountaineer*, signed H.B. but had subsequently been published and fully acknowledged on the editorial page of the *Montreal Star*.

> On tiny Magog's main street, then,
> There was a little shop, where I, aged ten,
> Would go for lemonade (the green kind's best!) –
> And listen to Ma Cameron with zest –
>
> Ma Cameron! who, innocent of guile,
> Would give us sips for nothing while
> We'd hear her tales of country fun and lore
> And always – almost always! – ask for more.

But Howie's most magisterial work had appeared in the potato-smelling pages of the *PAPT Teachers Magazine*. A footnote had identified the author as "poet and teacher of English." *The Moun-*

tain and the Cottage – A Sonnet had appeared between two articles entitled *Psycho-Drama and the Grade Seven Composition Programme* and *The Role of the Newspaper in the Classroom.*

> The cottage overlooks a lake I love
> And tea, and strawberries, and records try
> To wipe away the tears of years above
> The times we live in – but I cry
> O'er fields and meadows long since past
> And lift my eyes towards the skies of silver
> And see the shadow of the old black hill where
> Nature rolls her organ boom so vast.
> But oh! how sharp the lash that pricks my heart
> When Now and Then compare themselves for me
> As my old shades, in awful fragments, part
> And Churches, of my Mountain, say, "'Tis He!"
> 'Tis not God made my Mountain! Or my Lake!
> But Nature – whom I write for for Her Sake.

David sighed.

You didn't find stuff like that every day.

Yes, his throat was definitely sore. His bank of free Sick Days already overdrawn in bed with Susan.

Doctor's Certificate?

The Advantages of Apartment Dwelling.

Saddening.

Saddening. The moment free choice was offered, recidivists to a man. Chronic Reader's Digestion at sixteen, poor bastards.

David stared out of the window.

Oh, Constantimides, recent immigrant and novice teacher, how the heart ached for you at the year's beginning. Amid the chatter of the Merrymount Pre-Term Orientation Programme. "Constantimides," you said, "teacher of Physics and Office Practice."

"David Appleby."

"What," you said, "*is* Office Practice?"

The Advantages of Apartment Dwelling.

"A four-line filler on page thirty-one," said Jim. "Number forty-seven discovered last night. Tied up with barbed wire in the trunk of a car."

"Murders?"

"What the *Gazette* calls 'gangland slaying.' Wonder what they'd think of that in Sevenoaks?"

"Hey, Jim. I was meaning to ask you. Is it true you can hire thugs in Montreal to beat people up? Not other thugs – just ordinary people. I mean, is it a regular sort of thing?"

"I should think so. Why?"

"Oh, nothing. Just something Susan was saying the other week."

"They traditionally use baseball bats, I believe," said Jim.

"Mmmmm."

"And a pretty safe line of work it is, too," Jim said. "Last year in Montreal general crime solution ran at roughly 21% and crimes of violence at 17%. Which would tend to argue . . ."

Letters fell through the flap and plopped onto the lino. Jim jumped up and went down the passage to get them. David heard him tearing a letter open.

His peculiar horror, he decided, was not so much arms or legs but broken teeth. A club in the mouth.

"How about some tea?" Jim called.

"If you're making it."

As Jim filled the kettle, he was whistling. Chink of cups and saucers. He started singing. He brought the tray in and put it on the floor between them.

"Well," he said, "it's up the bum of the Greater School Board and up the joint bums of Noddy and Big Ears. Up *theirs,* mate. Right up to the oesophagus."

"How's that, then?"

Jim tapped the letter sticking out of his shirt pocket.

"Just in time to save me breaking contract."

"What are you talking about?" said David.

"The OISE offer. Which is satisfying because it's unwise to leave a mess behind you."

"What are you *talking* about? What's oisy?"

"I told you I was applying, didn't I?"

"For *what?*"

"Oh, I thought I had. For the Ontario Institute of Studies in Education. It's in Toronto."

"You didn't say anything about it."

"I've been accepted to do a Ph.D. and I've got a grant of $4,200."

"No, you never said a word about it."

"$4,200," said Jim. "With what I've got saved and if I get some consulting at Research Associates in the summer – perfect."

"So, you're going away, then," said David.

"September," said Jim. "August, more likely. But there's no problem. The lease is up here and you can move to a smaller place. And if you moved near Merrymount, you wouldn't have travelling expenses."

"No, I suppose not," said David.

"And the really good thing, you see – I've been accepted under Bellheimer which means I can take my pick when I'm finished."

"Who's he?"

"American. Maladjustment. Very big deal."

"Oh," said David.

"I reckon I can make $3,000 this summer if I push it at Research Associates – I'll have my M.Ed. so they'll have to pay me more. Then there'll be two years pension money back from the government – that should be eight or nine hundred."

"Well, congratulations, Jim. I hope it goes O.K."

"Yes, thanks. You won't have any trouble finding a place, you know. If you moved out towards Merrymount you'd have to pay more than sharing a place but rents are cheaper out there."

Jim sat on the arm of his chair and opened the letter again.

"Yes, I suppose they would be," said David.

"What?"

"Rents."

Jim went into his bedroom and came back knotting a tie.

"Think I'll go up to McGill," he said. "Potter about in the stacks. I'll have to read all Bellheimer's bloody books now."

"I suppose I'll have to call you 'Dr. Wilson' in a couple of years," said David.

"I shall insist on it," said Jim. "Tie straight?"

"Yes."

"I saw that friend of yours at the library last week," he said, putting on his jacket. "The fair-haired guy at Merrymount."

"Garry?"

"Yes, he's doing the introductory statistics course with Noddy."

"What for?"

"Starting an M.Ed."

"I didn't know Garry was doing that."

"He's going into guidance. It's what *you'd* do if you had any sense. Another degree of some sort, anyway."

"Are you sure? He's going to get the Head of the History Department when Follet retires. Grierson more or less promised him."

"What's a department head make?" demanded Jim.

"*I* don't know."

"No, *you* wouldn't. Seven-fifty over scale. Peanuts."

"Well, why's guidance any better?"

"Don't you *ever* notice the way things operate?" said Jim irritably. "You've worked for the Board for two years now. You get into guidance – and you do some administration in that, right? Kardex Cards, time-tabling, organizing photographs for bus-passes – right? And if you're efficient, the Board uses that as a selection process for its vice-principals. Jesus Christ, you irritate me sometimes!"

"Hadn't thought about it," said David.

"I'm off," said Jim. "I'll buy you lunch at *Carmen's* if you like."

"No. No, I can't, Jim. I've got to get these bloody papers finished for tomorrow."

"See you, then."

When the front door had closed and Jim's footsteps had sounded away down the stairs, David sat in the silent apartment looking at the letter on the arm of Jim's chair.

Sunlight on the strewn sheets of the *Gazette.*

Jim's empty cup.

Gothic candles surmounted by strawberry bakelite shades.

He traced the ballpoint round and round the islands of fabric on the grease-smoothed arm of the old chair.

The street was suddenly loud with children.

He picked up the papers and sat the pile on his knee again.

Run-on sentence.

SP.

Logic?

Punc.

Oh, Constantimides, Constantimides, teacher of Physics and Office Practice!

How the heart ached for you at the year's beginning.

Lapels festooned with badges, thirty ballpoints bristling, Ronnie Biggin was marking the register when David walked into the classroom eight minutes late.

"As you were late, sir . . ."

"Yes, thank you."

David dumped the envelopes of exam papers on the desk. He had managed three hours sleep.

"Shall I carry on, sir?"

Officious little prick. An embryo clip-board man.

While Ronnie officiated, David muffled the intercom apparatus with his jacket, turned the picture of the Queen and the Duke of Edinburgh to face the wall, and, taking down the Canadian flag which hung to the side of the blackboard, stowed it in the bottom drawer of his desk.

Williams, Henry?

Zazlowski, Charmaine?

Who had taken advantage of first-day confusion to appear in a knit dress; she smiled at him. Breasts like . . . what fruit could compare? He gave her a jolly smile.

Satyriasis?

"A note for you, Mr. Appleby, sir," said Ronnie Biggin.

Chairs are to place on desks. Windows are to close
and lock by gold thing on top. Floor dirty.

> George Dimakopoulos
> *Janitor.*

"Thank you," said David.

Just before the holiday, he had bought two copies of *The Family of Man* and mounted most of the photographs on the pieces of cardboard that came back from the cleaner's with his shirts. He'd hoped that some of the pictures might spark memories or feelings which he could fashion in his composition lessons. It was not for a couple of minutes that he noticed the gaps in the rows.

He walked round noting what was missing.

Missing were photographs of:

a boy and girl lying in the grass kissing

a sailor with two girls

a pregnant woman lying on a bed

a pregnant woman looking out of a window

a baby being delivered

a woman breast-feeding

a bare-bum African boy hurling a spear

a family group of Australian aborigines.

Enquiry would be merely ritual. He felt irritated but too tired to bother. The bloody kid who took them must have been in a really bad way. Why couldn't he have stolen *Nightstand* books from a cigar store or peered at underwear ads in *Cosmopolitan?* Even the *Ed Sullivan Show* was raunchier than a group of shrivelled, dug-hanging aborigines.

While Ronnie Biggin distributed the exam papers, David slumped in his chair staring towards the window remembering suddenly Ossie Prosser. Ossie, thirteen or so then, masturbated countless times a day, storing the proceeds in a *Brylcreem* jar which he flashed to the class whenever the master was writing on the board. They'd watched him carefully for the legendary signs of divine retribution, but Ossie, though pale, had not succumbed.

Young boys were grubby. Poor sods.

Still, it was irritating that the sequences, the comparisons and contrasts of the photographs had been spoiled.

"Right!" said David. "Settle down. Your exam. I was not pleased by your performance on the essay question. And I am being polite."

But by the last period in the morning David was in a savage mood. His stomach was eating itself; he felt sick and dizzy with coffee; hot grit grated behind his eyes.

He had been harassed by Miss Burgeon; a wad of forms he distinctly remembered having thrown in the garbage before the holiday. He had promised them for the afternoon.

He had been pressured again by Visual Aid to hand in outstanding monies for the Year Book, monies he had spent. He would have to approach Jim for a loan.

He had been pestered by the Secretary about the mathematics of his last monthly register-total.

His free period, the one following recess, had been taken away by Grierson who had commanded him to muster two hundred kids to form an audience for a visit from the McGill Chamber Orchestra. Grierson, forced by Board policy to suffer these cultural intrusions from time to time, had instructed him not to disturb regular classes but to press only Practical Classes and the basement inhabitants of the Wood, Metal, and Auto Shops. These retardees had then been regaled with a programme of Bach and Vivaldi while he and three of the basement men walked the floor trying to prevent whistles, groping, match ignition, and loud speculations on the sexual habits of the lady cellist.

The bell had released him to teach his third class of the day.

"You have no occasion to talk while reading a poem," he said. "And I would be obliged, Alan, if you could chew with your mouth closed."

He decided to cut the lesson five minutes short so that he could get down to the cafeteria and secure an egg or cheese sandwich; although he needed food, he could not face a *May West* or bologna.

He glanced down at *Anthem for Doomed Youth* and wished he didn't have to talk about it.

"And each slow dusk a drawing-down of blinds."

He'd always been moved by that.

"What's 'orisons,' sir?" said Brian Inglis.

David pointed to the pile of dictionaries on his desk.

Udashkin was studying the *Gazette's* sports section.

West was completing what looked like geometry homework.

"Is that it?" said David.

"What?"

"Do you intend looking it up?"

"Oh," said Inglis. "Yeah."

The knock and the opening of the door were simultaneous. In the doorway stood McPhee.

"The class need not stand," he said.

"Yes, Mr. McPhee?" said David.

McPhee did not answer. In the chill silence, his eyes searched for signs of mutiny.

"Inglis," he said. "When I came in, were you out of your seat?"

"Yes, sir. I was getting a book from Mr. . . . ."

"We've met before, haven't we, Inglis?"

"Yes, sir."

"Yes, sir," repeated McPhee.

There was a long silence.

"Are you chewing, Goldberg?"

"Yes, sir."

"Get down to my office."

McPhee picked up the poetry text, *On Wings of Song,* from the nearest desk and looked at the name written in the front. He stared at the girl. The girl blushed. Suddenly, he wheeled on the boy behind him and said,

"You! What class is this?"

"11E, sir."

McPhee nodded slowly as if something had been confirmed for him. He stared round the frozen room again and his gaze came to rest on David's jacket which was hanging over the intercom apparatus.

After long moments, he said,

"Can I have a word with you, Mr. Appleby?"

"Carry on with the poem," said David.

They went out into the corridor and McPhee closed the door after them.

"I waited for you in my office during recess, Mr. Appleby."

"Waited for me?"

"Are you in the habit of ignoring your mail?"

"Oh," said David. "I was rather rushed this morning. I haven't checked it yet."

"I had asked you to see me in my office as I thought the privacy would be more appropriate. However. I'd like to . . ."

He opened the folder he was carrying, squared a sheet of paper with his fingertips.

"Look into a couple of matters. Brought to my attention."

Sparrow cockings of his head.

"Did you set a composition assignment in grade ten to be completed over the holiday – an assignment called *The Medical Examination* or *The Dentist?*"

"Yes," said David.

"Those were the actual essay titles?"

"Yes, that's right."

"And is it true that when discussing this assignment in the last week of last term you mentioned being naked and the production of urine samples?"

"Probably," shrugged David. "I don't really remember. Why? What's this about?"

"You don't wish to deny this?"

"No, of course not."

"Do you consider it normal to ask students of fifteen to write about undergoing a medical examination?"

"Certainly. Much more normal than asking them their views on capital punishment or the future of the United Nations or something."

"So this particular assignment, as far as you were concerned, was a normal and typical part of your composition programme?"

"Well, 'programme' suggests rather more organization than . . ."

"But you would consider it typical of your . . ."

"Well, in that it's aiming at the same general sort of purpose."

"I see," said McPhee.

"Why?" said David. "What's the problem?"

"I see," repeated McPhee. "The problem, Mr. Appleby, is this."

He opened the folder and turned the corners of the four pieces of paper.

"Letters of complaint from three parents."

"Why?"

"You're asking me *why*, Mr. Appleby?"

"Yes. What can they possibly . . ."

"Over and above *that*," said McPhee, "we have also received a call about the unsuitable photographs exhibited in your room."

"Oh, no!" said David. "You're joking!"

"As I was bound to do," said McPhee, "I investigated the matter. During the holiday I removed some of the photographs – those I considered unwise or in poor taste."

"*Poor taste!*"

"What, exactly, do you think you're trying to *do*, Mr. Appleby?"

Light from the window in the classroom door caught both his lenses turning him into a mad scientist in a horror comic.

"Are you aware, Mr. McPhee," said David, "that those photographs are an internationally famous collection? That they were sponsored by one of the biggest New York museums?"

"Merrymount High School is *not* New York, Mr. Appleby."

"What's that mean?" said David.

"Let's return to the matter of this assignment . . ." said McPhee.

"Yes," said David. "Let's return to that."

"Mr. Appleby. I don't like your tone."

"I'm not enchanted by yours," said David.

McPhee was silent for a moment. He looked down at the folder. He opened the folder and closed it. He studied the combination lock on the nearest locker with a display of obvious patience.

"I am trying," he said, "to deal with this matter on an unofficial level. Grave though it is. If you are insolent to me, we will proceed differently."

David stared at him.

"You don't seem to realize," said McPhee, "that I'm trying to help you."

"I don't even understand what you're complaining about," said David.

"*Urine samples*," said McPhee. "Fifteen year old girls . . ."

"Look!" said David. "I'm merely trying to force my kids into writing about real things and real feelings in a real world. They all *have* medicals. Here, in school. I don't see what on earth . . ."

"You haven't yet been granted your Permanent Certificate, have you, Mr. Appleby?"

"No."

"No, I thought not."

There was a silence. The noise from the classroom was rising.

"Anyway," said David, "I don't know why you should place so much importance on letters and crank phone-calls."

"Crank?" repeated McPhee.

"Yes. Cranks and semi-literates. Good God! I mean, *The Family of Man*, it's one of the . . ."

"We exist," said McPhee, "to serve the community."

"So if some anti-evolution loony phoned you . . ."

"Don't bandy words with me!" snapped McPhee. "The area of sex is a sensitive one."

"Sex?"

"Photographs. Urine samples. Nakedness. This is a *school*."

"Those photographs aren't exactly from Port Said."

"I refuse to bicker with you, Mr. Appleby. My time is limited."

He tapped on the folder with his pen.

"I don't doubt your sincerity," he said. "Nor your concern for your subject. I'm making allowances for the fact that you are a young teacher from a different system – from a different country."

Where, in Montreal, David wondered, could one buy *tartan ties*?

"But I am forced to describe your attitude as misguided."

David waited.

"I feel that you're in need of some mature guidance at this point in your career and it's for this reason that I've asked Mr. Bunceford to visit your grade ten class to teach a demonstration lesson in composition."

"Bunceford!"

"*Mr.* Bunceford is your Head of Department."

"And what if our ideas of good writing clash?"

"Mr. Bunceford is older than you. He has been teaching for many years. The Senior Consultant in English and the Board have a high opinion of his capabilities."

"Well, I'm afraid *I* don't," said David.

"Your opinion is more valuable than that of the Consultant and the Board?"

David shrugged.

"Your personal opinion outweighs the Guidelines for Composition laid down in the Handbook?"

David did not reply.

A small blue and gold badge in McPhee's lapel.

"Everyone but you is out of step, Mr. Appleby? Is that it?"

Again David said nothing.

"Good," said McPhee.

He opened the folder again and checked a note on one of the pieces of paper.

"I have arranged for Mr. Bunceford to visit your grade ten class the last period this afternoon."

"I'm sorry," said David. "I don't find the proposition acceptable."

"It is not, Mr. Appleby, *a proposition.*"

They looked at each other.

"Do I make myself clear?"

McPhee turned and started down the corridor. Metal edges on his heels rang. At the end of the corridor, light flashed on the opening glass door.

". . . for what is life worth," said Howie, "if we have no time to stand and stare? What is life worth if, as the poet puts it, we have,

'No time to turn at Beauty's glance,
And watch her feet, how they can dance'?"

David, sitting on a desk at the back of the room, stared down at his shoes.

Fifteen more minutes.

Hands loosely clasped, looking like a minister inviting a congregation to prayer, Howie said,

" . . . and so I'd like to share with you, then, a beautiful descriptive passage written by the famous British author Sir Compton Mackenzie. Perhaps we can't all write so beautifully ourselves but we *can* all aspire to lofty goals, can't we?"

He smiled.

He opened the *Oxford Book of English Prose*.

"Quite, quite silent now," he said.

Eyes lifted to the sunlight at the tall window, he waited.

In unctuous voice he began to read.

"Some four and twenty miles from Curtain Wells on the Great West Road is a tangle of briers among whose blossoms an old damask rose is sometimes visible. If the curious traveller should pause and examine this fragrant wilderness, he will plainly perceive the remains of an ancient garden, and if he be of an imaginative character of mind will readily recall the legend of the Sleeping Beauty in her mouldering palace; for some enchantment still enthralls the spot, so that he who bravely dares the thorns is well rewarded with pensive dreams, and, as he lingers a while gathering the flowers or watching their petals flutter to the green shadows beneath, will haply see elusive Beauty hurry past . . .

"Here at the date of this tale stood the *Basket of Roses* Inn, a mile or so away from a small village.

". . . The *Basket of Roses* was the fairest dearest inn down all that billowy London Road . . .

"Old Tabrum the landlord was eighty years old now, with a bloom on his cheeks like an autumn pippin and two limpid blue eyes that looked straight into yours and, if you had any reverence at all, made the tears well involuntarily at the sight of such gentle beauty . . ."

David shifted on the desk.

"The ancient man was a great gardener as properly became a landlord whose sign was a swinging posy. What a garden there was

101

at the back of this florious inn. The bowling-green surrounded by four grey walls was the finest ever known, and as for the borders, deep borders twelve feet wide, they were full of every sweet flower. There were Columbines and Canterbury Bells and Blue Bells of Coventry and Lilies and Candy Goldilocks with Penny flowers or White Satin and Fair Maids of France and Fair Maids of Kent and London Pride.

"There was Herb of Grace and Rosemary and Lavender to pluck and crush between your fingers, while some one rolled the jack across the level green of the ground. In Spring there were Tulips and Jacynths, Dames' Violets and Primroses, Cowslips of Jerusalem, Daffodils and Pansies, Lupins like spires in the dusk, and Ladies' Smocks in the shadowed corners. As for Summer, why the very heart of high June and hot July dwelt in that fragrant enclosure. Sweet Johns and Sweet Williams with Dragon flowers and crimson Pease-blossom and tumbling Peonies, Blue Moonwort and the Melancholy Gentlemen, Larksheels, Marigold, Hearts, Hollyhocks and Candy Tufts. There was Venus' Looking-glass, and Flower of Bristol, and Apple of Love and Blue Helmets and Herb Paris and Campion and Love in a Mist and Ladies' Laces and Sweet Sultans or Turkey Corn-flowers, Gillyflower Carnations (Ruffling Rob of Westminster amongst them) with Dittany, Sops in Wine and Floramer, Widow Wail and Bergamot, True Thyme and Gilded Thyme, Good Night at Noon and Flower de Luce, Golden Mouse-Ear, Prince's Feathers, Pinks and deep red damask roses.

"It was a very wonderful garden indeed."

The insane shattering din of the day's last bell.

Howie stared down at the page.

David stared at Howie's pink pate.

When the clangour died, Howie raised his head.

"Yes," he breathed. "Yes, it *was* a wonderful garden, wasn't it?"

Reverently, he closed the book; softly laid it on the desk.

He looked up.

"Thank you, Mr. Appleby," he said.

"Thank you, Mr. Bunceford," said David.

He sat where he was while the chattering kids milled out of the door.

Bye, sir.

Afternoon, Mr. Appleby.

When they had all gone, he went and sat at his desk. The corridor was solid with noise – conversation, feet, shouts, piles of books dumped, the clang of lockers. He sat looking towards the window, unseeing, while the noise of locker doors and combination locks became further spaced, until the noises echoed in the emptying building, until the corridor was silent.

In the silent room, the buzz of an early fly working against the window-panes, the *tock* of the minute hand jumping forward on the electric clock.

Outside from the Staff Parking Area just below his windows came the sound of feet running, sudden yells, the smack of a ball against the brickwork.

He walked down and stood watching the three boys. The desk under his palm felt rough; carved into it were the words,

Who will suck me off?

Compasses, by the look of the workmanship.

A tall boy turning, jumping and plucking the football from the air, sprinting then for an imaginary touchdown. His yellow nylon windbreaker ballooning as he ran. David watched them through the double glass until they rounded the corner of the Metal shop.

Turning back to the room, starting with the back row, he began puttting the chairs up on the desk-tops. From desk to desk, placing the chairs quietly, squaring them, row after row, he worked towards the front.

Then he went back to the windows and pulled them down by the brass handles completely shut, locked them with the brass catches.

Going to the front of the room again, he started to erase the boards, working in short sweeps. When he had finished, he placed the eraser on the ledge. The yellow chalkdust on his fingertips revealed the whorls and patterns of his prints. He stood by his desk rubbing at the chalkdust with his thumb.

Chapter
Six

The strange noises rose again from the ventilation shaft. As if someone was attacking a radiator with a sledgehammer while groaning.
Ten-thirty; the sun was shining. As long as the bugger didn't start
singing again as he had last night. David pulled down the blind.

He wondered why his sexual activities seemed doomed to hysterical interruption. The bedsprings, the Scots lady, the wilful blind, the
afternoon on the Mountain when they'd been surprised by the con-
stable on his horse, and now – booming French-Canadian ditties
while *in medias res*. A bit bloody much.

But what would Gagnon be doing there again in the morning?
He didn't usually slop into view until midday. It was unlikely he was
actually *mending* anything. Unless he'd been there all night? Hammering on a steel door, larding the ground with terrified sweat. Trapped like poor old Edward in the dungeon-hole of Berkeley Castle.

Good.

Fat, noisy sod.

He remembered escorting a coach-load of delinquents to Berkeley
Castle in his first year as a teacher; "history field-trips" such excur-
sions were called. One element had promptly dropped his lunch down
the dungeon-hole. As a prelude. Later, he'd got his arm stuck down
a cannon-mouth.

The scene on the ramparts was vividly before him. The tugging
mass of boys. The professional helper among them – "He's *always*

causing trouble, sir." The snivelling trappee. The Custodian with the buckets of warm, soapy water.

Not, technically, a cannon. A smaller field piece. A culverin? A falconet?

David stretched. His exercised stomach muscles were sore. The thought of Gagnon immured in a ventilation shaft was pleasing. A touch of the Edward the Seconds was precisely what he deserved – a few inches of glowing poker up his arse. His just deserts for interrupting people.

Susan.

He hoped she'd make it home before twelve-thirty. The taxi had taken twenty minutes to arrive. All had been comparatively quiet on the Home Front; her mother had been praying for her again in St. Joseph's Oratory; her father had been jocular of late often shaking his head and saying, "Oh, that poor *shaykh*. I'm a rotten man, may God forgive me. I hope he got *Blue Cross*." On her bed, a magazine article, "Can a Young Woman Find Happiness With an Older Man: Twelve Personal Stories."

His ear, the hair round his temple, and the pillow were sticky. Pink. Pineapple Chicken from the *Nanking* Dinner No. 5 for 2. What was so romantic about eating from scorching hot cardboard boxes in bed?

This room must be cleaned.

Susan, golden in the glow of the electric fire, looking down at herself as she rubbed sperm over her breasts and stomach.

"It's good for the skin."

"Who said?"

"I did."

"It's sticky. And it goes cold."

"It's nice. Millions of babies."

A renewed outburst from the ventilation shaft.

"Displays of petulance will be punished," said David.

He got out of bed and went to the kitchen. Sunshine was warm on his chest. A good day for a walk on the Mountain. There was no bread. He looked in the fridge but did not fancy pickled pimentos or mayonnaise. He ate a mouthful of cold rice from the *Nanking* bucket but thought of maggots. He put the kettle on to make coffee.

Jim was out – probably buying the papers; or by this time he'd have taken them on up to McGill library. There was a full hour before Garry was supposed to arrive.

He took the mug of coffee into the living room. Facedown on Jim's chair was a Bellheimer book. He glanced at the first paragraph and saw the word "neonate." He looked it up in his Webster's. He nodded; he had suspected as much. He settled into his armchair; an hour before he need wash and get dressed. Garry was usually late.

Saturday mornings in Canada seemed just like Sundays in England – coffee, pottering about, paper-reading. But he did miss the *News of the World*.

Midnight was too violent.

What Canada lacked, he decided, apart from widespread eccentricity, was hundreds of quavering, senile, dotty magistrates.

"What, exactly, *are* 'panties'?"

Yes, thought David, centuries of culture and tradition.

Here, raw farmhands, driven mad by snow and bible-study, wiped out small communities in Northern Saskatchewan with .22 rifles. Perversity in England was more . . . mellow. One of his *News of the World* favourites, an exhibitionist who had been acquitted because he had not exposed his organ proper but merely a wickerwork facsimile strapped on and coated with cream cheese.

And the brave little man who had posed as a Municipal Health Department doctor and had gone all round a council estate in the mornings examining ladies' chests for TB. Before leaving each house he had always said,

"You'll be getting your little green book next week."

Genius. Pure genius.

It was not for several weeks that these women realized they had been the victims of a vicious assault . . .

Nostalgia swept over him.

Hunger, too.

Perhaps he could persuade Garry to go out for lunch? But Garry never seemed to have much money with him these days and often claimed to have just eaten. He was always in a hurry, having to leave places to pick June up or take her somewhere. Better to just phone out for something after they'd had a couple of drinks – and leave the phone off the hook.

He'd thought about it, tried to make sense of it, struggled to *feel* the relationship, until he'd just given up and chosen not to think about it at all. It couldn't be passion sweeping all before it, not with June. With her horsy teeth and drooping-pear behind. And they'd been married for six years anyway. And it certainly wasn't her qualities as a companion.

Garry was ridden by enthusiasms; last year it had been A. S. Neil and *This Magazine is About Schools* which had lit the wasteland of Merrymount for him; lately, he had been reading Franz Fanon and some obscure bore called Marcuse, both of whom he had tried to inflict on David. Between these major enthusiasms, Garry read Beckett and Pinter, Ken Kesey, William Golding, Norman Mailer . . . with his various jobs and the grotesque hours he worked, David didn't know where he found the time.

Yet June, the companion of his bosom, seemed to read nothing but *Glamour, Cosmopolitan,* and *Good Housekeeping*; poetry and novels were "serious" or "far too hard for me" – display of Macleans Teeth.

She emptied ashtrays between cigarettes and was jolly.

If you boys are going to work, you're only getting one beer each!
Jolly smile.

If Garry suggested a pizza or Chinese food, she always countered with offers of hot-dogs, and, if defeated, always contrived to be seen checking her purse.

Their child, a rather indeterminate four-year-old boy, was always being chauffeured to Creative Music for the Very Young, Painting Lessons, or to his Play Group.

As the hour wore on to eleven p.m. she excused herself and retired, always calling them "nighthawks."

Jolly smile.

At school, Garry described his eight-hour production of *Godot,* the school he would like to start, the Canadian history text he intended writing to teach kids about the Winnipeg Riots, the dumping of pigs and grain into the sea off Vancouver during the Depression,

"fuck the fur trade"

"that'd be a good title"

the internment of the Japanese and the theft of their property . . .

Garry's eyes shining with laughter, they elaborated the exploits of Sir Charles Pharco-Hollister, proposed dreadful final solutions of the McPhee, Bunceford, Grierson, Hubnichuk and Follet problems.

The afternoon they'd gone to a tavern and become drunk on laughter writing an elaborate Bunceford and planning to send it under Howie's name to the *Montreal Star*. The poem had been called "The Ruined Nest." He'd forgotten most of it now – last year, last summer – but the opening lines were,

> *Lo! In the crotch of a naked branch*
> *Behold the hairy Nest!*

They'd been eating peanuts, he remembered, hot from a vending machine; you'd had to catch them in a wax-paper cone. And that had been the first time he'd seen people putting salt in beer.

Yet the same Garry was married to June and supported that showroom, that glossy advertisement of a house.

June.

June of the inevitable stretch-pants and candy-stripe sneakers.

Tv-Mother of the flowered coffee-mugs.

David, a Pansy or a Snapdragon?

June of the Teak and anxious coasters.

June of the ski-slopes and keep-fit classes.

June of the coiffured friends whose first names all ended in "ie."

Juice-time, Chrissy!

June of the Budget.

June of the WEAK DRINKS.

And Garry supported it and her by teaching all day at Merrymount, by teaching two evenings a week at Sir George Williams High School, by tutoring rich half-wits, by slaving his summers away at an Educational Day Camp.

God!

Her body, her mind, even the whiteness of her teeth was offensive. All was sani-sealed. Asexual in her wholesomeness, like cheerleaders. The human equivalent of a slice of *Weston's* bread.

But Creative Music for the Very Young!

Oh, Fanon! Oh, Beckett! Were there *no* limits?

He decided that when Garry arrived, he'd get some very *strong* drinks into him and release Grierson's speech at Graduation, Grierson explaining to the Board's Regional Officer the necessity of using the per capita library allowance to buy new uniforms for the football team, George Dimakopoulos trying to seduce Miss Burgeon . . .

He drained the coffee, the bitterness of the last mouthful making him shudder. The sun was warm on his feet. He got up and looked along the plank and brick bookcase for something to read. There wasn't really much point in trying to think about the Garry thing; it didn't make sense, it really didn't make sense at all.

He considered a collection of *Playboy* cartoons, passed over a block of Jim's twaddly neonate and sibling books, settled finally on Chandler's *The Little Sister*. He sat down again and opened the book in the middle. It was falling to pieces; he should really buy a hard-cover copy. One of the American greats. It was obviously something he was going to read for years. He knew the plot so well that now he just read random chunks, savouring the writing, luxuriating in the awful similies. Dashiell Hammett was good – no one denied Chandler's debt to him – but Hammett just didn't sparkle as much. It was no use arguing about it. Garry was quite wrong.

She stood so that I had to practically push her mammaries out of the way to get through the door. She smelled the way the Taj Mahal looks by moonlight.

David almost sighed with pleasure.

When the doorbell rang, he was still undressed, still reading. He walked down the passage and opened the door. Garry's arms were piled with books and rolls of drawing-paper.

"Garry! Listen to this."

She had pewter-coloured hair set in a ruthless permanent, a hard beak and large moist eyes with the sympathetic expression of wet stones.

110

"Isn't that fine?" said David. "*Chandler*, asshole!"

"Your hallway and the stairs *smell*," said Garry.

"You get used to it. It's Gagnon. What's all that stuff?" he asked as they walked into the living room.

"The books you lent me. Couple of others."

"And what are these scroll things?"

"Ah!" said Garry. "Those are the answer!"

"Oh, Gawd!" said David. "They weren't dictated to you, were they?"

"I've got it pinned down, Dave. I *know* I'm right. The last act eh? Remember last Thursday – we just weren't getting any spark there?"

"The Alice and Peter bit?"

"Right. Remember how soggy it was? Well, I've got it – it's the actual *physical* distance between them. And they back off each other anyway – you notice they're still doing that? But, look!" said Garry, choosing one of the rolls of paper.

"Let me get some clothes on," said David. "Won't be a minute. There's some scotch on the counter in the kitchen."

When he came back, Garry had one of the rolls spread over the arms of Jim's chair, the corners held down with books.

"It was pretty dead, eh? Now look at this! All we've got to do is move the counter to *here*. Right? And have Alice out from here to *here*. What do you think?"

David looked at the diagram.

"First night's Thursday, Garry. We can't rehearse new patterns in three days, for Christ's sake!"

"But what about the idea?"

"Yes, you're probably right."

"It isn't as much as you think."

"But there'd be the movements for the cops, too."

"I've got that," said Garry, tapping one of the rolls.

"Well, when could we do it?" said David.

"Monday after school – and here's another thing. An uncle of mine died today and I've got to go to the funeral – I'll be away all day Tuesday because it's in Ontario. In Brockville. So you'd have to do it on your own on Tuesday."

"And we can't touch them on Wednesday. . . ." said David.

"What do you think?" said Garry.

David looked at the diagram again.

"Think we can work it?" Garry said.

The doorbell rang.

As David went down the passage he said over his shoulder,

"I hope your uncle wasn't . . ."

"Hardly knew him," called Garry. "It's one of those family things —my mother . . ."

David opened the door and saw Susan.

"Hi," she said

David grimaced and shooed at her with his hand.

West-lake, he mouthed.

"What?" said Susan loudly.

"Is that Jim?" called Garry.

"Westlake!" whispered David.

"Oh, Christ!" whispered Susan. "Look, I've got this . . ."

Someone gave a loud moan.

"What's . . ."

"Is it?" said a slurred voice. "Is it the place?"

Garry came down the passage.

"Oh," he said. "Hello."

"Hi, Mr. Westlake," said Susan.

"And what can we do for you, Susan?" said David.

"I remembered you said once you lived on this street, Mr. Appleby, near St. Mark, and I've been going from apartment to apartment looking at the names and it's been awful . . ."

"Is it?" said the voice. "The place . . ."

"Who's that?" said David.

"It's this man . . ." she said.

David and Garry went out onto the landing and looked round the corner at the man sprawled on the floor.

"I was with Frances Campbell and we were drinking Cokes and reading the magazines in a laundermat and he came in and he was dancing," she prattled, "and he took this woman's clothes out of the drier and he was trying to put a bra on and a policeman came . . ."

The man rolled onto his side and drew up his knees.

"And he fell down and did that to his head and we said he was with us because the cop was going to arrest him and then later he wanted to go in a bank and it's Saturday and he started waving his arms and Frances took off and I didn't know where to go . . ."

The man groaned.

"I'm sorry if I . . ."

Her voice trailed away, almost childishly.

"No, that's O.K. Don't worry about it," said David.

Garry bent to look at the man's face.

"What a mess!" he said.

Behind him, Susan crossed her eyes and jabbered her tongue in and out.

David frowned at her.

"I didn't really know what else to do . . ." she said.

The gash on the man's forehead looked like shallow lips. The crust of blood was dark brown but thick beads of crimson stood along the centre of the cut. His black suit was dishevelled and dusty, his white shirt stained with blood on the collar and front. He looked about thirty years old, short brown hair. He was gripping a black leather briefcase on which was stamped in gold the initials W.P.C. On his finger, a big square ring. His left trouser leg was rucked up, revealing a short black sock and a few inches of white leg.

"Well . . ." said David. "I suppose we'd better get him inside."

"Can you take his bag, Susan?" said Garry.

"He won't let go of it," she said.

"Is he basically . . . friendly?" said David.

"Sure," she said. "His name's Bill."

"You take the other side, Garry."

They struggled to hoist him to his feet. He was heavily built and about six feet tall. They got him upright and propped against the wall. His head hung. The black bag pulled him down.

"Bill?" said David. "We're going into the house now so you can rest. Do you think you can walk?"

"Was he like this before?" said Garry.

"No," said Susan. "Just since he was lying down."

"Bill?" said David.

"This is the place, Bill," said Susan. "O.K.?"

He stiffened and forced his head up.

"If I've offended you," he said slowly, "want to apologize."

He swayed forward and Garry pushed him back against the wall.

"Susan, can you get the door? Garry."

They struggled down the passage and dumped him into David's armchair, arranging his limbs as if he were a lay-figure. He still gripped the black bag. They stood looking down at him.

"It'll be more comfortable on your knee," said Susan, lifting the bag.

"We'd better clean that cut," said David.

"We ought to phone for an ambulance," said Garry. "He needs stitches in that."

"But if he goes to hospital like this, won't they arrest him or something?" said Susan.

David shrugged.

"I wonder if there's anyone we can call?" said Garry.

"Look, I think we ought to clean that," said David. "He's too drunk to feel anything.

"Maybe if he's married . . ." said Garry.

"Yes, he is," said Susan. "He said that every morning his wife vacuums the sheets to get rid of body hair."

"*What?*" said Garry.

David cleared his throat.

"Bill?" he said quickly. "What's your other name? What does the 'C' stand for?"

The man stared at him and then slowly fumbled into his top pocket and got out some cards. Garry took them from him.

> *William Payne Collins*
> *District Representative*
> *Monksford Pharmaceuticals*

114

"Well, that's not much help, is it?" said David.

"We could call his company, I suppose," said Garry.

"But he'd get into trouble," said Susan.

"He might have concussion or brain damage, Susan," said Garry. "I'm not trying to sell him for thirty pieces of silver. Look at his colour."

"Where do you live, Bill?" said David.

"We should get an ambulance," said Garry.

"Tell us where you live," said Susan.

He got his hand inside his jacket and groped into his inside pocket. He brought out four plastic ballpoints and held them out to Susan, indicating Garry and David.

"Compliments," he mumbled.

She handed them each a pen.

On the pens was a caduceus crowned by a large M. Underneath the caduceus were the words,

A Nation's Health . . .

"This is *ridiculous*," said Garry, sitting down in the rocking chair.

"I'm sorry," said Susan, "but I didn't know where else . . ."

"I'm going to clean that," said David.

The man's eyes were closed; his head lolled.

"Can I do anything to help, Mr. Appleby?"

"How about making some coffee all round?" said David.

She started towards the kitchen.

"Kitchen's down there on your right," said David. "Cups and coffee in the cupboard over the sink."

"Yes," said Garry, getting up and choosing one of the rolls of drawing-paper. "Give him some coffee. Perhaps he'll dance again."

He sat down in the rocking chair and spread the diagram.

"Well, it might buck him up a bit," said David. "He's very white-looking."

He got warm water and cotton wool from the bathroom and started to soak off the dried blood around the cut. Trickles of water cut clean paths through the dirt on the man's cheek. He did not open his eyes. Susan brought in coffee on a tray.

David held the man's head up while Susan held the cup. He tried to turn his head away.

"Drink some," said Susan. "You'll feel better."

They managed to get half the coffee down him.

"That cut's not as bad as it looked," David said.

"Needs stitches," said Garry from the rocking chair.

The front door opened.

"Oh, Jim!" said David as he came into the living room. "This is one of my students from Merrymount, Susan Haddad, and you know Garry, don't you?"

"Hello," said Jim, nodding round. "And who's that?"

"That," said David, "is William Payne Collins. And he's paralytically drunk. Susan found him in a laundermat and thoughtfully . . ."

The man suddenly started to struggle into a sitting position. His breathing was loud and heavy. He dropped his black bag on the floor. David and Susan and Jim stood watching him.

"What the hell's he been drinking?" said Jim. "Gasoline?"

Grunting now, the man worked himself forward to the very edge of the chair. Suddenly, he tipped forward from the waist, as if severed, and spewed on the floor.

"Jesus Christ!" said Jim. "This is intolerable!"

He walked out and his bedroom door slammed shut.

The man hung there, a string of drool spindling from his parted lips.

"Heigh-ho!" said Garry.

"I'm really, really sorry, Mr. Appleby," said Susan.

William Payne Collins began to snore.

"O.K.! O.K.!" said David. "That's it. There's no point in trying to do anything with him. We'll dump him on the floor and leave him till he wakes up and then he can go to a hospital or home or the nearest bloody bar or whatever the fuck he . . ."

Susan came back from the kitchen with a bowl of water and a sponge. She started cleaning up the spattered vomit.

"Garry?"

They heaved him out of the chair and stretched him out on the floor beside the bookshelves. David undid his collar and pushed a cushion under his head.

"I don't think it'll stain much," said Susan. "It's mainly the coffee."

"On this carpet," said David, "it couldn't matter less. Scrub much harder and you'll be through to the floorboards."

"Got any air-freshener?" said Garry, opening the window.

"I feel really awful about it," said Susan.

"Well, don't," said David. "It's not your fault he threw up. And it doesn't matter anyway."

"But I brought him here," she said.

"It's perfectly O.K. Susan."

"We'll probably get to like him," said Garry.

"I ought to pour this down the toilet," she said.

"On your right," said David, pointing.

When she came back into the living room, she said, "I put some bleach in the bowl and left it in the tub. I don't think it'll . . ."

"It'll be cleaner than it's ever been before," said David.

"Well . . ." she said.

"Yes," said David.

"I suppose I'd better be going . . ."

"O.K.," said David. "And don't worry about him. He'll be just fine when he wakes up. Sadder but wiser, as they say."

"Bye, Mr. Westlake. And sorry I disturbed you."

"Goodbye, Susan."

David walked down the passage and opened the door for her. As he did so, she puckered her lips at him in a mimed kiss; in reply, he rolled his eyes heavenward. Then pulled back quickly as she brushed her hand against his cock.

"Bye, Mr. Appleby."

"See you on Monday," said David as she started down the stairs.

She wasn't wearing a bra again.

"Well . . ." said David, as he went back into the living room.

"Incredible," said Garry.

"Never a dull moment, as they say," said David.

Garry closed the book he'd been looking at.

"If you'd asked me," he said, "which single kid in Merrymount would be most likely to find a transvestite drunk in a laundermat and take him to a teacher's house, Susan Haddad would have been my first choice."

"Ah, well," said David. "It's all part of life's rich pageant."

Garry shook his head.

"And her friend as well," he said. "What's-her-name. Frances! I mean, what other kids go to laundermats to read old magazines?"

"Actually," said David, "she's very bright. They both are."

"Sure," said Garry. "She's probably the brightest kid in Merrymount. I had her last year for grade ten history. But it's all *wasted*."

David shrugged.

"She never did any assignments," said Garry, "just sat there reading novels."

"Good novels?"

"Umm?"

"Who *is* this speaking?" said David. "Surely not Our Man from Summerhill?"

"Oh, for Christ's sake!" said Garry. "That's got nothing to do with it. It's a matter of intelligence. We're already operating *in* a system – and the way she behaves – well, it's just *unintelligent*. She'll probably flunk her matrics if she's carrying on the way she was last year."

"Well," said David. "It's her funeral. I don't suppose there's much you can do about it."

"It's the *waste*," said Garry. "Ever seen her Cumulative Record?"

"What, Kardex things?"

"*And* the file in guidance. Incredible. Trouble right back to grade six. Bright as hell, but you can't do anything with her. You ask Brunhoff for that file sometime – drunk in art classes, a gallon of wine found in her locker, breaking into McPhee's office with one of the West Indian kids . . ."

"When did she do that?"

"Oh, this was all grade eight. Imagine!"

"Why did they . . ."

"Stole the strap and the punishment-book and then – yeah, O.K. –
but it isn't really all *that* funny," said Garry.

"Highly public-spirited," said David.

"Yes, O.K. In one way it is, but . . ."

"We should put her forward for the Lamp of Learning Award:
Special Services."

"But it's not an isolated thing, you see. It's part of a pattern. And
don't forget that breaking and entering was involved."

David pulled a serious face.

"They stole money, too," said Garry. "And then she's run away
from home three times and there've been two arrests under-age in a
licensed jazz-club, suspected drug-use. It just goes on and on. You
take a look sometime. A real self-destructive pattern."

"Neonates," said David.

"What?"

"Psychology text-books."

Garry shrugged.

"It's all there," he said. "Promiscuous, too, if you can believe the
books."

"Well, I don't know," said David. "I rather like her."

"Me, too," said Garry. "She's an attractive person. And she's damn
good-looking. But just be a bit careful, that's all."

"How do you mean?"

"Well, coming to your apartment and that sort of thing. She's a
student and you're a teacher."

David pulled a face.

"It puts you in a vulnerable position," said Garry.

"You were here," said David.

"People talk, you know," said Garry. "She tells a few kids she was
at your apartment . . ."

"Oh, come on!" said David.

"You didn't know Pete Russell, did you? He was at Merrymount
three years ago. He went to Ottawa on the bus with the Senior Girls
Basketball Team and he was sitting next to one of the girls on the way
back. That's all. Chatting to her. But rumours started about him and

the Board transferred him at the end of the year. And the *next* year, his contract wasn't renewed. He'd been inspected a lot and they suddenly discovered he was incompetent."

"Typically shitty of them."

"Sure," said Garry. "But that's the way it is. And *please* don't tell me it shouldn't be."

David said nothing.

"Oh, I know what you're thinking," Garry said. "You think I'm being cautious and petty and anti-human and . . ."

"Look, I didn't say . . ."

"And you're damn right! I'm married and I've got a kid."

"Fair enough," said David.

"It's the *one* thing," said Garry. "A whole career . . ."

David nodded.

"Christ!" said Garry. "Some of those guys at Merrymount won't even see kids alone in their classrooms unless the door's wide open. Did you know that? Girls *or* boys."

"I suppose you're right," said David.

"Each to his own," said Garry.

David nodded.

There was a silence.

William Payne Collins burbled on.

"Still," said Garry, "no damage done."

"Anyway," said David, "how about a scotch?"

"Quarter to two," said Garry. "No, I'd better be moving."

"A small one," said David.

"No," said Garry, getting up. "I've got to pick June up at her mother's and we're supposed to be going down to Eaton's."

"You haven't time for a quick lunch? A sandwich?"

"I'll take a raincheck," said Garry. "Look, about the play. Think about it and take a look at the diagrams and call me tomorrow? If you think it's O.K. we can get a Monday evening rehearsal put on the Bulletin."

They went down the passage to the door.

"God, it smells out here!" said Garry.

120

"So," said David. "I'll call you on Sunday. Tomorrow."

"In the morning," said Garry.

"See you, then."

Garry turned on the stairs and said, "If we do it on Monday, we won't be finished before seven, seven-thirty, so would you like to have supper with us afterwards?"

"Fine," said David. "Thank you."

"And then I can give you a lift home."

"Perfect," said David. "I'll look forward to it."

Garry saluted, and was gone.

Chapter Seven

❀

The bell rang.

The day's last class began to drift in.

With the opening performance of *Night Haul* at eight p.m., David found it difficult to concentrate on teaching. And the exam was squatting on his mind; a day and a half to go. It was beginning to look as if diarrhea would have to strike tomorrow.

Sitting on the desk in front of him were copies of *The Teacher's Handbook for Use in Quebec Protestant Schools* and *Early Days – A Memoir* – the prescribed texts for the Permanent Certificate exam. He had been carrying them all day. On Saturday morning he would be sitting the exam for the third time. But *this* time he really intended reading the books. During the course of the day, he had mastered two pieces of information: the legal maximum of chairs allowable in one classroom and the best methods of assisting in developing good attitudes to health.

Early Days – A Memoir was still defeating him; in numerous attempts he had never got past page five. It appeared to be the maunderings of some senile dreary who'd been an Inspector of Schools.

During recess, Follet had again said the word "thespian."

His free period, during which he'd promised himself to hack through "The High School Literature Course" in the *Handbook,* had been frittered away –

In Grades VIII and IX a minimum of 200 lines of poetry will be

selected for memorization, and at least 250 lines in Grades X and XI.
Principals are required to keep on file a list of the poems to be memor-
ized annually in each grade –
frittered away in chat with Miss Adams and in straining to overhear
a lecturer from Macdonald College instructing a student-teacher.

An inoffensive lad who'd been suffering from mononucleosis and
was obliged to make up his legal number of practice-teaching days.
The lecturer, a gaunt, earnest-looking gentleman with a huge, gulpy
Adam's apple, had advised the lad not to sit down or lean – such
postures belied the desired dynamism; to enquire from time to time
if his voice was audible; to be more relaxed; to grip the chalk, not
like a pen, but like a stick. These defects had been recorded on a
printed form which the gentleman carried on a clip-board.

David had been very interested.

Frittered away, frittered away.

By the end of Grade X students will know what is meant by ellip-
tical sentences, parallelism, emphasis, unity and coherence.

Highly comical.

He had forgotten that Thursday was his duty-day in the Cafeteria;
he had been reminded by Visual Aid.

"We've all got to pull together, you know."

He had patrolled the Cafeteria overseeing the proper disposition
of wrappers, paper-bags, crumbs, slices of salami, fruit rind and bread
crusts; he had prevented RUNNING.

The first lesson after lunch had been blessedly disturbed by a Fire
Drill.

"Come on!" said David, closing the *Handbook*. "Hurry it up!"

With a little less than five weeks to go before the Matrics, and as
most of the kids absented themselves for the last two of those weeks
anyway, he had bowed to their demands for revision, though he had
no intention of giving them the kind of revision they wanted. While
George and Miriam handed out the mimeographed sheets which
supplied all the bowdlerized material, David glanced through the
questions at the back of the Quebec Authorized Edition of *Two
Solitudes* – an edition "Arranged for School Reading and with Intro-
duction, Notes and Questions by Claude T. Bissell M.A. Ph.D."

Question Four was his favourite.

Marius is a study in abnormality. In Section 5, does MacLennan adequately account for his attitudes and actions?

A judicious question. A question, David decided, which for sheer nerve, was worthy of some form of award.

As Marius was motivated by guilty lust for his stepmother and hatred of his father for screwing said stepmother the night his first wife died, and, as both facts had been bowdlerized entirely in Section 5, the question indicated an advanced lack of shame on the part of Claude T. Bissell M.A. Ph.D.

Or possibly a black sense of humour?

When the class settled, David began to work through the deletions indicating where in the Authorized Edition they began and ended. He resented the wasted time – the classtime and the background labour of comparing the two editions; he resented the shameful expense of spirit in having been ineffably charming to Twatface to get the stencils typed; he resented having had to reward her with a 2 lb. box of *Black Magic* ($4.40). It wasn't fit work for a grown man.

He hadn't taught North American Literature before but had enjoyed most of the course. It was a great improvement over the Canadian History which he'd been forced to teach last year. Though looking back now, he supposed he was lucky to have escaped Office Practice.

"But Mr. Grierson! The men from the Board
   assured me in England that . . ."

"Bit of variety."

"But I don't know any Canadian History."

"Read the book."

"But . . ."

"Time-table can't be changed."

"But how . . ."

"A Good Teacher can teach anything."

Fresh off the boat, uncertain of the location of Vancouver, he had instructed thirty-three young Canadians in the history of their country.

"and so"

thrusting at vast masses of water with his pointer
"they followed the river route in *this* direction . . ."

A nerve-wracking year. Although Garry's expert lessons had carried him through announced visits, there had always been the danger of snap inspections. To counter this, he'd been forced to wage a year-long campaign of intimidation.

Follet had married money; he was a proud member of the Royal St. Lawrence Yacht Club.

David had played Cowes.

Against "our country place" he had played "roughshooting" over "the home farm" with rabbit pie at the "Dower House."

And so on.

His best stroke had been accidental. He'd been talking to one of his classes about typography and the next day had brought into school a book he'd bought on a market stall in England for a couple of shillings. A history of Monmouth's Rebellion printed in 1723. He'd never read it, but the print was nice. He'd dumped it on a coffee-table with some other books at recess and Follet had said,

"A lovely old volume!"

"Just something from the library at home," he'd replied.

Follet had been reduced to nodding and turning the pages.

"Next!" said David.

"Wait a minute, sir!"

"Ready?" said David. "The next one is Page 63."

The image of Kathleen's lush body still brimmed in his eyes and he felt sick from shame.

He wondered who was responsible for these prurient obscenities. The Ministry of Education in its larger wisdom? Claude T. Bissell M.A. Ph.D.? The Macmillan Company of Canada Limited? A monstrous cabal of deranged Confessional Committee members, Consultants in English, and the nation's Buncefords? Or a sickly, quivering web of the whole lot?

Garry had hold him that MacLennan lived in Montreal and taught at McGill and he had formed a picture of him as an old man, lonely, walking on the McGill lawns under old trees feeding the pigeons and squirrels with breadcrumbs from a paper bag. He didn't know exactly why he imagined MacLennan in this way. But the picture was quite clear. He filled the paper-bag every night ready for the morning. He always wore an old mac. He often stood watching the football practice, a figure apart from the shouting groups of students.

He wondered if MacLennan cared, if he had acquiesced in this butchery of something he must have loved. Or had it all been done to him? Betrayed by small print.

"Mr. Appleby?"

"Yes, Carl?"

"If we use this information on the exam, will we be penalized?"

"What do you mean? Why should you be?"

"Well, we're not supposed to be reading it and maybe the Examiner'll take marks off."

"And Mr. Appleby?"

"Yes, Mary?"

"What if the Examiner hasn't read the book – the proper one, I mean?"

"Put a note on your answers that you're referring to the complete text."

"But if we want," said Carl, "we can just refer to the school edition?"

David looked down at the wad of purple, mimeographed sheets.

"Yes, Carl," he said, "you can do that if you want."

He wiped the sweat from his face and forehead with his sleeve. The physics lab had been so designed that with the blinds down it was impossible to have windows open. The heat, the noise, the tense, excited chatter were beginning to make his head ache.

"Is that it?" said Alan.

"Yes, you're finished," said David.

He dropped the powder puff back into the box and wiped his hands on the rag. His back, too, was aching from stooping over upturned faces. He lighted another cigarette and stood looking round as Alice settled herself on the stool and tucked the towel into the neck of her blouse.

The room seemed jammed with kids again – cast, stage-crew, car park boys playing with torches, friends of the cast, ushers and usherettes in their red blazers, friends of friends. Radios were playing; the blond boy who operated the tape-recorder was strumming on his inevitable guitar. They'd cleared the room three times since six o'clock but there seemed no way of keeping the kids out. A crowd had gathered round Garry watching as he powdered Peter's hair. One of the truck-drivers was smoking a cigar; the two police officers were subduing the prompter. Nadja, a large butterfly barrette holding her dark hair at one side, was tarting about in her waitress costume; her skirt seemed to be getting shorter every time she passed by. Alex, the other truck-driver, was up at the far end of the lab glancing at his script and then staring at the balances in their glass cases, his lips moving.

"You two!" yelled Garry. "Stop that dancing! We haven't got time to work on you again."

David belched silently, tasting again the Canadian Meat Pie. He dropped the cigarette end into the sink nearest him and scooping up a dollop of cold cream, started to work it into Alice's hairline.

"Will you SIT DOWN!" yelled Garry.

Nadja pulled a face at his back.

. . . *can't even fix yourself a sandwich without suckholing round that man.*

"Ears," David said to Alice, "neck, and backs of your hands."

"Mr. Westlake says can he have the No. 18."

"What?"

"The No. 18 for Mr. Westlake."

David wiped his hands and passed the box to the boy.

"O.K.?" said Alice. "Mr. Appleby?"

He turned back to her and touched her cheek with his fingertip.

"Too greasy," he said. "Work it in some more."

"Sir?"

Someone coughed close behind him.

"Mr. Appleby?"

David clenched his teeth. Bruce Hannam. He let out his breath and turned to look at the boy.

"I know you're busy, sir, but we have a problem."

He had dressed himself for the evening in heavy work boots, jeans, a leather jacket, and a leather pouched harness which was festooned with screwdrivers, pliers, wrenches, shears, steel measures and staplers.

"Thought I'd better report it, sir. Number Three's on the blink."

He looked like a Bell linesman called out during an earthquake.

"Well," said David, "there's only forty minutes to go. We're all relying on you, Bruce."

"Don't worry, sir. I'll do my best. I should be able to fix it."

"Good lad," said David, nodding.

He turned back to Alice as Bruce clanked away.

He stood looking down at her.

He dabbed on spots of the sallow base, working it smooth with his fingertips. The waitress's white nylon coat whispered as her head and shoulders moved. Over the left breast in large red letters ANNA.

Twenty-five years of serving coffee and hamburgers, of greasy dishes and insufficient sleep; twenty-five years that would break this night into anguished speech.

He wiped his hands clean on the ragged towel and checked the time. He rooted around in the untidy box for the dark rouge and, placing a tiny spot low on her cheek, began to blend it into the base.

The cook positioned behind the cash register, the two truck-drivers, Anna facing the motionless police.

Resting his left forearm on her head, he started to hollow her temples with a brown liner.

The lights make it different.

Well you don't have red cheeks down there.

He stood back considering.

It makes her look like this — look.

"Do you think — you know, we're going to be all right?"

The shorter policeman moving down the counter; Anna moving diagonally to face the truck-drivers.

"You're going to be just great," he said, moving in to work brown shadow between the root of the nose and the eye-sockets.

"Just great."

Smearing maroon liner on a toothpick, he started to etch in the frown lines. Her breath moist against his wrist. Slowly. Delicately. The lines sharp. The two truck-drivers staring at her. Holding his breath as he worked was making his head throb.

Look, lady . . .

My name is Anna. Slap my ass, why don't you? Call me "Baby."

A white liner. Another toothpick. Each wrinkle highlighted with a line of white on each side.

He stepped back, staring at what he had done.

Powder would bring it down.

"Smile, Alice!" said a voice behind him. "You're on Candid Camera!"

David shouted.

Rounding on the grinning boys.

"Get out!" he shouted. "Get out of here!"

The wings were dim, a single pool of light in the centre of the stage. He stood staring; the light seemed to swim down to meet the boards.

He rubbed his finger over the end flat; rough, crystalline; Mr. Healey's Practicals had mixed in too much size.

He sat down and leaned back on one of the metal chairs, the cold bar pressing against his neck. His head was throbbing with each beat of his heart. He gazed up the cathedral heights of curtain.

He became aware of a dim figure in the shadows at the far side of the stage, a figure which clinked and clanked as it moved. He eased the chair down. He would not, could not face the No. 3 stepped-lens gambit, the pretext of the ellipsoidal-reflectors. Quietly, quietly down the steps and out into the corridor again. He wandered along towards the staffroom.

Very good, Hannam. Give of your best. Carry on.

Thank you, sir.

Earnest, helpful, horse-faced, a hairy mole on his chin, the inevitable president of the United Nations and Current Affairs Club.

Membership: seven.

With each block of lockers, each classroom passed, Bruce Hannam's life extended, more of the same. Always on the fringe of groups, tolerated, the man who was relied upon to collect monies, give lifts, address envelopes, count votes, staple papers, mend and fix. The man who at parties went for more ice.

David pushed open the door of the deserted staffroom. The red light glowed on the coffee urn. He looked round at the plastic palm tree in its brass-bound tub, the soiled patches on the empty chairs where heads had rested, the grey blankness of the television screen on which at lunchtimes they watched sporting events, lunar landings and Arab-Israeli wars. He sat down in his usual place on the settee near the wall-phone. Above his head the Disney-coloured trees of *Eaton's* Canadian Fall.

After a while he got up and went to his Home-Room. He sat there smoking cigarettes, tapping the ash into the little boat he had fashioned from the silver paper in his cigarette packet.

Dimakopoulos had centred the blotter on the desk. Brown mock-leather frame, green blotting paper. In the centre of the blotter, three books. He moved *Early Days – A Memoir* and *Two Solitudes* aside, and taking *The Teacher's Handbook for Use in Quebec Protestant Schools*, walked along the silent corridor to the physics lab. Someone had wedged both doors open; the room was empty.

He sat on the stool the kids had used. The dark brown bench-top was dusted with powder; he wiped a patch clean with a soiled Kleenex. He chucked the white, maroon and brown liners back into the make-up box. He turned to the section in the *Handbook* on English Language and Literature.

Not only does choral speaking stimulate interest and deepen appreciation but this approach to poetry is also an aid in developing clear enunciation and voice control.

He turned on the tap and held a toothpick in the jet. Water went up his sleeve. On the next bench, a green jacket, a copy of *Night Haul*, a pile of school books. He dried the toothpick with a Kleenex and used it to write his name in the powder on the bench. He drew a face, scribbling in a tangle of curly hair. Then he rubbed the name and the face away with a piece of cotton wool.

The educational value of dramatics is everywhere recognized. Voice control, poise and self-discipline are developed. Dramatics can also lead towards social maturity and insights into the art of the dramatist.

He wandered up to the end of the lab and looked at the balances in their glass cases.

On the board a kid had written "Beatles for Ever."

A heavy weight was hanging from a wire which was attached to a hook in the ceiling.

All he remembered of physics was being caned for reading *The Golden Bough* while he was supposed to have been lowering a brass weight on a string into a big glass calibrated tube. And attaching a length of rubber tubing to the tap and then inserting the other end of the tube into someone's pocket. Or had rubber tubes been chemistry? He set the heavy weight swinging.

He wandered back to the stool and the open book.

The teacher should accept every opportunity to plan his classroom techniques in such a way as to guide the development of character and citizenship. By taking part in group activities based on the course of study, children may be led to acceptable ways of working with others and to the development of habits of self-control, honesty and obedience.

Applause.

He looked up towards the open door.

Applause sounding, sounding from the auditorium.

Chapter Eight

❀

David lay naked and sweating on top of the sheets. The ticking of the *Jock* alarm-clock filled the room. Not even a draught stirred through the apartment. He peered at the clock's faint, luminous glow; the hands seemed to be pointing to one a.m.

It was the first hot night in June.

Bloody country.

A choice between being staked out in a Turkish Bath or hobbling around with frostbite and piles. In England, summer would have set in with its usual, sensible, severity. A mosquito whined near his ear. He slapped at the noise and banged his knuckles on the wall.

He sat up in bed and punched the pillow up behind him. He lighted a cigarette and flicked the match out of the window. His next apartment was going to have screens on the windows; and normal heating; and garbage disposal of some conventional kind. And it wasn't going to have Monsieur André Gagnon yelling *Tête carré!* behind you as you went up the stairs.

He leaned out of bed staring at the clock; ten minutes past one. It was something at least that he wasn't on till the afternoon. Morning was Technical Drawing; he was Biology. He'd been looking forward to Matrics but had forgotten that the boredom of invigilating was more tiring than teaching. After he'd read the exam-paper, the Fire Regulations on the wall, studied the notice-board and any charts there might be in the room, after counting the cars in the Staff

Parking Area if he was lucky enough to be on that side, after tallying them by colour and size because he didn't know any makes except *Volkswagen*, he was left with the students and their ritual gestures; the ceiling-scanners, the pen-suckers, the blotters, the pickers of thoughtful noses, the hand-hoverers, the cuff shooters, the bra-strappers, the hair-twisters and/or pullers. By the last hour he was reduced to trying to see up girls' skirts.

Thirteen more days to go – or was it fourteen – till the end of term. All he had left to do, apart from invigilation, was the one set of grade ten report cards and his register.

The register; that was going to be a problem. And the apartment. And England. He must remember to ask the boys in the grocery for cardboard boxes.

He still hadn't decided about the holiday; it was a choice between England and New Orleans. His mother and father were expecting him but he hadn't said anything definite. He could ride Greyhounds down to Knoxville, Nashville, Memphis, New Orleans, hear some blues singers, see the country.

He turned the pillow to its cool side and tried the words again quite casually, as if in conversation.

"The summer? Oh, I rode Greyhounds down to Nashville, Memphis, on to New Orleans ..."

Or possibly "rode on Greyhounds"?

The very word "Greyhound" excited him; it linked him to the fabulous, mythic world of the blues, the shining trumpets. It worked the same poetry on him as *levee, County Farm, grits, bull-fiddle.*

He felt himself smiling.

Remembering a line from an old blues;

I've been to the Nation and roun' the Territo'

He'd never wanted to know what it meant.

Yes.

And then there was all the passport business. His was expired and he'd need photographs and forms. But he could get into the States with the piece of landed-immigrant paper they'd given him on the ship. And then there was finding a new apartment and moving; whether to get a place and pay for it over the summer or find a place when he came back. And if he found a place when he came back, there was the problem of storing things over the summer. Where?

With Garry?

He resolved to make a list of things to be done. The lease was up at the end of the month. Tomorrow he'd definitely make a list. During Biology. The knowledge of the mosquito was making him feel itchy all over. Sleep was impossible.

He put on his dressing-gown and went into the kitchen. The light inside the fridge was off again. There was just enough milk for breakfast. They were out of Chinese tea. No lemons. He ran the cold water tap. The fridge motor sounded loud in the silence. The tapping at the door made him start. He tightened the cord of his dressing-gown and went down the passage.

"Susan!"

"Can't stop. I've brought you a present."

"Where've you been?"

"Chinatown. With Fran."

"But you've got Biology tomorrow . . ."

She plucked off her sun-glasses and kissed him. A short, sleeveless black dress, the Chinese jade disc clinking against its chain. Her mouth was hot.

"I've got a cab out front."

"You look beautiful," he said.

"Here. For you."

"And inebriated," he said.

She pushed the crumpled shopping-bag into his arms. Leaning in, crushing the bag between them, she kissed him again.

"It's for you."

"What is it?"

"It's because I love you," she said. "Talk to you tomorrow."

He listened to her heels clattering down the stairs.

"After you, my dear Alphonse!" she called.

In the kitchen, he opened the bag and put the four parcels on the counter. The first was flat and about a foot square. He unwrapped the sheets of newspaper and saw a sign which said:

Keep Off the Grass

By Order

Fresh earth clung to its stake.

The second parcel turned out to be a packet of joss-sticks, a paint-brush, and a gold lacquer box which contained a block of Chinese ink.

The third parcel, wrapped in tissue, contained a small dried fish.

The fourth was a pineapple.

Chapter Nine

❀

As he neared McPhee's office, David considered.

He'd faked his register but most people did that. Year Book money? His additions to the Detention Book? But he'd printed in block letters. The poem! Attributing the poem on the grade ten exam to Sir Charles Pharco-Hollister.

He went into the General Office and through the swing-gate at the end of the counter. Twatface looked up from her typewriter and smiled.

Black Magic. $4.40. *And* on school time anyway.

He smiled back at her.

Past Miss Burgeon's office.

Perhaps it was for showing *Some Like It Hot* without prior clearance. But that had been three weeks ago. There had, apparently, been phone calls.

The safe.

McPhee's office, the door half-open. He knocked.

"Ah, Mr. Appleby. Come in. I think that one's more comfortable."

He closed the folder and got up to put it in the green filing cabinet. The drawer rumbled shut.

"Enrolment projections," he said.

David half-smiled, nodded.

"You've been invigilating since nine," said McPhee.

"Yes," said David.

"Well, I expect you could use a cup of coffee?" McPhee smiled.

"Thank you, yes," said David. "I certainly could."

"They call it 'elevenses' in England, don't they?"

"Yes, that's right," smiled David.

"We're just on time then. I'll go and have a word with Mrs. Simmons . . ."

David took out his cigarettes; he hesitated and then lighted one, dropping the match into the clean ashtray on McPhee's desk. On the wall above the green filing cabinet, a print of Van Gogh's *Sunflowers*.

On the wall just above his head there was a School Board calendar. He counted the number of black squares left before the red of the holiday.

The Greater Montreal Protestant School Board.

GMPSB

Gumpsbub

Gumpsba.

"Well," said McPhee, coming back into the room and seating himself at the desk, "I've been meaning to have a word with you for the last two days but the Matrics seem to . . ."

He brought out a folder from his desk drawer; he opened the folder and studied the top piece of paper. David watched him. He was wearing a dapper brown suit today and a yellow tie which was decorated with brown fox-heads and black horse-shoes. David remembered a tie something like that when he'd been about ten; definitely fox-heads. But had it been *green* with *red* foxheads? He tried to reconstruct the top of his dressing-table, the one he'd had then. McPhee sniffed. Elephant ebony bookends. One with a broken tusk replaced with a matchstick. A tortoise-shell comb with a silver back.

"I understand," said McPhee suddenly, "that you were successful this time in your Permanent Certificate exam?"

"Yes," said David. "I heard the following week."

"Yes," said McPhee. "The Board's Regional Officer – you've met Mr. Sharp, haven't you?"

"No," said David, "I don't believe I have."

"So now there's only a final Principal's Report."

"Yes, I suppose so," said David.

"And you've been with us now for two years, Mr. Appleby."

"Yes," said David. "That's right."

"And you've been teaching for three?"

"One year in England," said David.

"Born in Southbourne. England, in 1944," McPhee said, putting the sheet of paper back in the folder.

"Which makes you twenty – "

"Three," said David.

"And how are you liking Canada?" said McPhee.

"Oh, very much," said David. "Very much indeed."

Twatface came in with a tray.

"Ginger biscuits today, Mr. McPhee," she said.

"You spoil me, Mrs. Simmons," he said.

She smiled at him; the dress yellow and Doris Day.

"Thank you, Mr. McPhee," she said as she closed the door.

"Thank *you,* Mrs. Simmons," said McPhee.

He indicated the tray.

"Cream? Sugar?"

David spooned sugar into his cup and stirred.

"I've been meaning to talk to you," said McPhee, proffering the plate of biscuits, "about your relationship with the Haddad girl."

David forced his hand to keep moving forward, his fingers to close around a Ginger Snap.

"The Haddad girl?" he said.

"Susan Haddad," said McPhee.

"Relationship?" said David.

"Some months ago," said McPhee, "we received a phone call from the girl's mother claiming that Susan was involved in an undesirable relationship with one of her teachers."

"But *I'm* not one of her teachers," said David.

"I'm aware of that," said McPhee.

"And this woman said *I* ..."

"No," said McPhee. "She didn't know the name of the teacher involved."

"It sounds rather odd to me," said David. "What did she mean, exactly?"

"At the time," said McPhee, "it sounded odd to us. Recently, however, the matter has come to our attention again. A concerned staff member has placed evidence before Mr. Grierson that your relationship with this girl is more than the relationship between teacher and student."

"What evidence?"

"Quite correctly, in my view, the staff member concerned felt that the nature of your relationship was not in the best interests of the school, the girl, or the profession."

"Well I don't know *what* to say to that, Mr. McPhee. I really don't know what you're talking about. What is this 'evidence' supposed to be?"

"Do you deny a relationship with the girl?"

"Our relationship is a very warm and friendly one. She's the most intelligent student I've ever talked to. What possible . . ."

"You see her outside the school situation."

"I have done," said David, "on occasion."

"You admit that?"

"A cup of coffee sometimes," said David.

"A cup of coffee," said McPhee.

"What do you mean by that?" demanded David. "What exactly are you accusing me of, Mr. McPhee?"

"Accusing, Mr. Appleby?"

"Are you suggesting that my friendship with the girl is improper? Because that's certainly what I'm understanding you to mean. Is that what you're implying, Mr. McPhee? That the relationship is a sexual one?"

"Mr. Appleby! I'm quite sure I have made *no such statement.*"

"You've certainly made such implication."

They sat staring at each other.

"I would like to know," said David, clattering his cup and saucer back onto the tray, "who has accused me of this and on what evidence."

Moving aside the jug of cream, McPhee set down his cup.

"Mr. Appleby," he said, shaking his head slowly, "Mr. Appleby. We're not in a court of law here and I'm not accusing you of immoral conduct. Nor was the staff member concerned."

"And just who *is* 'the staff member concerned'?"

McPhee spread his hands.

"Teaching," he said, "is a delicate profession."

He started to twist the wedding band on his finger.

"A school . . . I like to think of a school as an organism – or a *fabric* – a fabric of which we're all a part. I think you'll be able to understand why we feel we must protect the staff member's confidence. But I do assure you that the staff member did not accuse you of – it was certainly not the spirit in which the information was offered."

"An accused person," David said, "has the right . . ."

"A delicate profession," repeated McPhee, raising his voice. "It appears, Mr. Appleby, that your reports from the Department's inspectors are very favourable indeed. Both Mr. Bunceford and Mr. Follet have spoken highly of your capabilities and your range of knowledge. It would seem, too, judging from what I've heard and from the Year Book that you are popular with the students."

"Thank you," said David. "But I'm more interested in . . ."

"Allow me to continue," said McPhee.

"Let's get back to this 'concerned staff member' and this 'evidence,'" said David.

"*It would seem*," said McPhee. "Thank you, Mr. Appleby. It would seem that you are standing on the threshold of a promising career. Yet we must balance against this your behaviour and your *attitude*. A very *minor* example," said McPhee, indicating the corner of his desk.

"Pardon?" said David.

"Most staff members," said McPhee, "men much older and more experienced than you, would not smoke uninvited in my office."

David stared at him.

"Not, in *itself*," said McPhee, with a dismissing wave of his hand, "but there are other matters."

He opened the file again.

"Look here!" David said. "You're accusing me . . ."

"Absent seventeen teaching-days, late twenty-three sessions," read McPhee. "Duties missed – fourteen. A heavy burden, Mr. Appleby, on the rest of the staff."

He turned the page.

"There have been incidents. The photographs in your classroom; the matter of your essay assignments; that strange behaviour on the first floor with a water-pistol; unauthorized screening of movies; a lack of co-operation with the Visual Aids Department – Mr. Clements has reported to me on several occasions. Continual complaints from Mr. Dimakopoulos who claims that your classroom is the untidiest in the school and who also reports to me that he finds ash and cigarette ends in your garbage can. Smoking in the classroom at the close of school contravenes the Fire Regulations. There is a staffroom for your comfort and convenience."

McPhee looked up.

"Do you find the staffroom uncongenial?" he asked

"What do you mean?"

"You find it difficult to get along with your fellow-teachers?"

"Not at all," said David.

"Miss Leet has complained to me on two occasions of your rudeness to her. On the last occasion she was weeping."

"She's hysterical," said David. "It was a clash of opinion over literary matters."

McPhee raised his eyebrows.

"About a writer called Ayn Rand."

"But the point at issue," said McPhee, "you're the only teacher against whom I have heard such complaints."

David shrugged.

"Then," continued McPhee, "we received further information – and a listing from *Mrs. Lewis* . . ." He turned sheets of paper in the folder.

"Yes."

He lifted a typewritten sheet and shook it straight.

"Library books," he said.

He frowned as he scanned the page.

He glanced up.

"Well?"

"But staff can keep books out until the last day of term, can't they? Wasn't there a notice . . .?"

"Can you recover them?" said McPhee. "Our information is that you've removed a substantial number."

"Substantial?" said David.

"I chose to use the word 'removed,' Mr. Appleby. In spite of the fact that the books were being used by Merrymount students for educational purposes, I could have chosen an uglier word."

He slapped the folder.

"Well, Mr. Appleby?"

He tilted his chair backwards.

"It was just a matter of speed, really. You see I wanted those particular students . . ."

"A sorry record!" said McPhee.

"And I most certainly had *no* intention . . ."

"A sum," interrupted McPhee, "apparently in excess of $230."

"If I may just explain . . ."

"I expect," interrupted McPhee again, seeming to stare at the GMPSB Calender above David's head, "that you're aware of the mechanics of contract renewal within our system?"

"Yes," said David.

"That, if by April 30th, no indication to the contrary has been received by either party, then the previous year's contract is automatically renewed?"

"Yes, I know," said David.

"You are, then, presently under contract for the coming year."

David nodded.

"Contracts can be terminated by the Board, however, for behaviour which falls under any one of three defined areas."

There was a silence. David concentrated on the brown fox-heads, the black horse-shoes.

"Of three," repeated McPhee, "defined areas."

David studied the cups and saucers, the facets of the cut-glass cream-jug, the chrome apostle-spoon.

"Doubtless," said McPhee, "you are aware of the nature of those areas."

He pursed his lips.

He edged the file square on the desk with his fingertip.

"We *are* understanding each other aren't we, Mr. Appleby?"

"I think so," said David.

"Today," said McPhee, "is . . .?"

"Wednesday," said David.

"Wednesday," repeated McPhee. "Let us say, then, Friday – at the close of afternoon school."

"What?" said David.

McPhee circled the appointment on his desk-diary and looked up.

"I don't wish you to make hasty decisions," he said. "I would like you to have the time to consider your position carefully. On Friday, I will require you to promise to end your relationship with the Haddad girl and to avoid any such attachments in the future. If you feel unable to comply, I have been authorized to offer you the chance to resign."

"I don't need two days to . . ."

"Friday," interrupted McPhee.

"What do you think I . . ."

"NO, Mr. Appleby! I wish *you* to think. Calmly."

He stood up.

"At three o'clock," he said.

David stood up and turned to leave.

"Oh, perhaps . . ." said McPhee. "If you could just look at this general list compiled by Mrs. Lewis and indicate those titles . . ."

David took the proffered typewritten sheet.

McPhee handed him a ballpoint.

"*Now?*" said David.

"Thank you," said McPhee.

Chapter Ten

Jim, clad in his underpants, was wedged into his armchair, his legs over the arm, reading *Time Magazine*.

David sighed.

"I wish you'd stop doing that," Jim said.

"What?"

"That sighing. I'm *trying* to read."

"Sorry."

David got up and went to the window; the running bands of colour dyed the night sky over Ste. Catherine Street – red, green, yellow, red again. Soon the nighthawks would be coming back from wherever they went to, the white bars on their wings just visible as they dived through the light above the sign in pursuit of insects. He remembered a pair of them he'd seen last summer at twilight up near the cemetery, climbing and suddenly falling in great slides and swerves down miles of sky.

"*And* that," said Jim.

"What?"

"That bloody tapping!"

"I'm *terribly* sorry!"

"Oh, Jesus Christ!" said Jim, throwing down the magazine. "Come off it, will you!"

"Come off what?"

"I thought we'd finished this last night."

"Come off what?"

"This fucking *Byron* act all over the place."

He clapped one hand to his naked chest and declaimed in a Shakespeary voice.

"Do your worst, fiendish McPhee, for the depth of my love will not allow me to betray it!"

"Very witty," said David.

"I'm sorry," said Jim. "I'm not in the mood for all this bathetic crap again. All this 'betraying our relationship' stuff. I've had a hard day. Profitable though," he added. "Profitable."

"O.K." said David. "So you're trying to read. I'm sorry."

"Oh, fuck off!" said Jim. "You needn't go all wounded either."

"I wasn't aware that I was."

"Well you are," said Jim.

There was a silence.

"You're not contemplating anything *bizarre*, are you?" said Jim. "Starting with a flourish sort of thing? I mean, you don't want to *marry* her?"

"No," said David. "But that's not the point."

Jim shrugged.

"*Is* it?" said David.

"For Christ's sake!" said Jim. "What are you 'betraying'? You're still going to go on seeing her whatever you say to McPhee. All that, well, it's just *mummery*. So play it out. You won't *mean* what you say and he won't *believe* what you say. Right? And everyone's happy. So tell me – *explain* to me – what, exactly, are you supposed to be 'betraying'?"

David stared at him.

"Go on. I find all this very educational. Tell me."

"I told you last night," said David.

"You *emoted* rather tediously last night," said Jim. "But tell me again. It's the workings of your mind. Fascinating."

David shrugged.

"All you're saying," said Jim, "is that you don't want to kiss McPhee's arse."

"Maybe."

" 'Maybe' bebuggered!" said Jim. "You know what you've got, mate? An aversion to the old *osculum infame*, that's all. Not that you've much choice."

"Why?"

" 'Yes sir, yes sir, three bags full, sir,' and you're away."

"Why haven't I much choice?"

Jim groaned.

"How much have you got in the bank?" he said.

"Not much. Twenty dollars or so. I can get a job."

"Doing what?"

"With another Board maybe. Or a private school."

"Thought of the Arctic, have you?" said Jim. "Department of Indian Affairs probably isn't too fussy. Anywhere in this province and they're going to get on the phone if you haven't got references. *Young guy called Appleby. Ah! Really? Gets into their panties, does he?*"

"Well, I was thinking – I could say I'd just come from England. It'd mean dropping two increments on the scale, that's all."

"Well have another think," said Jim. "The Department's got you and so has the PAPT. Letters of Standing and your Certificate exam – all that stuff. Wouldn't work."

"Shit!" said David. "You're right, I hadn't thought of that. And would it be the same for a private school?"

"Probably. Most of them get provincial grants and they need certificated teachers for that."

"But not all of them?"

"You might get away with it in Ontario," said Jim. "Probably would. But you wouldn't get a job in Toronto – that's policy. If you'd fancy living in some hick town and going to sugaring-off parties or bowling or whatever the hell they do."

"Well, I'll look for some other job then."

Jim gave a sudden snort of laughter.

"Did you ever meet that guy Fletcher at my school?" he said.

"Don't think so."

"Always wears silk suits, clammy hands. Smiles a lot."

"No. Why?"

"I was just thinking. That first winter. God, was I embarrassed! He came up very confidentially and he said, 'A few of the guys are planning a sugaring-off party and we wondered if you'd be interested?'"

"*Sweetie!*" said David.

"Like a Terry Southern thing," said Jim. "All starkers with great, hairy sugar-coated dongs."

"Rude," agreed David.

Jim scooped up the *Montreal Star*.

"Do you want *Time*?" he said, chucking the magazine across.

"But there must be *something*, Jim! Advertising or something."

Jim shook out the Classified section.

"The old parlez-vous'd be the problem for you, wouldn't it?"

"Well you don't need it for everything," said David.

SKILLED HELP

"That's out for a start," said Jim.

"You know you said most private schools get provincial grants? Are there some that don't? Where I could try the straight from England thing?"

SERIOUS *man for wholesale fish company.*

"Are there, Jim?"

"Look them up in the Yellow Pages."

STEADY *work for mature drivers.*

David opened *Time* and stared at an advert for *Old Clipper* whisky.

What did one do?

Start with a photograph and then write words to fit?

HORIZONTAL *boring mill operator.*

The whole idea offended him.

I drink Old Clipper because it makes me drunk!

"Here's a splendid one for you," said Jim.

BODY MAN *urgent.*

"Where *is* the phone-book?" said David.

"Your only other miscalculation," said Jim, "is that they won't be

148

hiring teachers in the summer and they'll probably have hired completely for next year anyway and your salary would end next month."

David slapped the magazine shut.

"Hmmmm," said Jim from behind the paper.

$150 PER *wk. Car provided.*

"Would you describe yourself as 'aggressive,' " he went on, "and 'customer-oriented'?"

"No," said David.

"No, I wouldn't either."

"What about language schools?" said David.

$100 WKLY. *draw against commission. Free training, free parking.*

"Oh, shut-up!"

"Trouble with you, mate," said Jim, "you're unskilled, unilingual, too old, over-educated. . . ."

"How about some tea?" said David.

"If you're making it. You know," said Jim, tapping the paper, "you could put one of these in yourself."

UNILINGUAL CHILD-MOLESTER, *intellectual interests, seeks opportunities teaching, other.*

As David stood in the kitchen by the open window looking out on the jungle of pipes and the iron grills and ladders of the fire-escape, he thought of a drink; of drinking. The back of his palate dry and sour. Rum. Rum for a hot evening. Trinidad rum. Ice with four ounces of *Old Oak.*

From Old Oaks great notions grow!

Definitely one for the glossies. One like that every day and he'd be earning $50,000 a year.

Mauve pigeon shit on the window-sill again.

The Quebec Liquor Board employees were still on strike. The bars were running the stuff in from Ontario but the thought of getting dressed and going out and seeing people and having to talk perhaps – all too depressing. The kettle was coming to the boil.

Getting dressed to go out drinking. Ludicrous.

Cheap melodrama.

Like fat Harry Seagoon hammering on the door of the den of vice in the Indian Quarter of Bombay. The Street of a Thousand Households.

where a man may drink and forget his sorrows. . . .

He slammed the kettle back onto the stove.

"Hey, Dave!"

"What?"

MESSENGER, *5-day wk. bicycle provided.*

Taking the mugs into the living room, he said,

"But what *I* don't understand – they had me two ways. Why the hell didn't they just fire me?"

"Not their style, old son," said Jim. "Not their style."

David smiled and raised his sandwich in salutation as John Gardener ambled through the Common Room and on into the Men's Staff-room. John smiled his vague smile and waved. He'd be invigilating in the last of the Matrics. Latin. Seven students. Sixty-nine years old, he'd been brought out of retirement for one class a day to burnish Bunceford's efforts. David smiled. When Hubnichuk or Follet or McPhee talked at him, he turned off his hearing aid and stared at them like a bewildered baby; when irritated by his students he lowered his voice to an inaudible mumble. Once in a staff meeting, while Grierson had been outlining the Board's revised policy on hair and uniforms, he had suddenly said in a loud voice,

"Would anyone care for an apple?"

He lived alone in an apartment downtown and spent most of his time translating Latin poetry into rather bad English verse. David and he had fallen into the habit of going out to dinner together a couple of times a month.

David always steered him home, taking his arm at crossings so that he didn't jar himself stepping off the curb. In his apartment, they always drank cognac and the old man always played the harpsichord – the *Two and Three Part Inventions*, the *Little Notebook* – until his fingers began to stumble. And then he talked about his childhood in Ontario and his wife whose harpsichord it had been. Sometimes he recited Latin poets and lectured David on prosody, sometimes talked of his travels, the war, the family house near London, long since sold.

His face would become reddened, his speech more and more slurred, and then David would put him to bed, working off his shoes, peeling the hot socks from his puffy feet, getting him between the sheets in his underwear.

Then he would work the false teeth from the slack mouth and put them in the glass of water on the bedside table; turn the old man's head to one side on the pillow and put out the light. Before letting himself out, he always emptied the ashtray and washed the snifters in the cramped kitchenette; always filled the electric kettle and put it beside the bed with a cup containing instant coffee and sugar.

Neither of them ever mentioned the evenings they spent together and John was always formally pleasant the next day.

David wondered how he could stand wearing a suit and a waist-coat on a day like this; habit, upbringing? Perhaps at that age one always felt cold.

Grit. David winced. She hadn't washed the celery.

The Cafeteria woman was what Canadians called "ethnic" – a strange usage. French, English, or Americans were French, English, or American; Serbs, Estonians, Greeks etc. were "ethnic." Presumably a euphemism for "immigrant" or "foreigner." But whatever, she was bloody weird. The prospect of the end of term had produced a frenzy of odd sandwiches; she'd mixed tuna fish and cream cheese in this one, studding the result with chopped celery.

As David ate, he watched Henry Bardolini who was sitting at the other end of the long coffee-table counting out nickels and pennies and arranging them in little ten-cent stacks. The proceeds of his daily Stamp Club meeting. He opened his *Samsonite* briefcase and checked through one of his little cellophane books of stamps. The compartments of the case bulged with packets and books of stamps, packets of sticky hinges, used envelopes, and promotional literature for the *Wonder Book of Universal Knowledge*. He was reputed to own an apartment building in Notre Dame de Grace and a smoked-meat shop on St. Lawrence. He taught French.

"HI THERE, HENRY!" boomed Hubnichuk, barging through the swing door from the Men's Staffroom.

"WHAT DO YOU SAY, DAVY-BOY!"

"eight, nine, *ten*," said Bardolini deliberately.

Hubnichuk dropped himself into the armchair opposite David.

"Well," he said, slapping his meaty hands on his knees, "thank God it's Friday!"

David nodded.

"Yes sir!" said Hubnichuk. "T.G.I.F."

Oaf.

Ethnic-face.

"Guess it must have been a smart move with the play after all," he said.

"Ummm?"

"Shifting it from the second term to the third."

"Oh," said David.

"Hear you cleared a profit," said Hubnichuk.

David nodded, smiled.

"WELL!" said Hubnichuk slapping his knees again and getting up.

Cries, laughter, exclamations, a general twittering going on from the group of women round Miss Britnell. As Hubnichuk passed them, he bellowed, "TO WORK, LADIES! TO WORK!" David saw the brochure pass from hand to hand. He had seen a copy of it at recess. Hills, horses, a golf-course with electric carts to ride about in, a bar, a man in a Stetson tossing a pancake, a group singing round a bonfire . . . *tired but jubilant. The nitely Bar B-Q and songfest led by Luke, our trailboss.*

Stringy Miss Britnell, senior and aged Phys. Ed. mistress, had joined forces with Miss Burgeon and Miss Leet to spend the holiday on a dude-ranch in Montana.

David glanced at the clock above the door. Five minutes past one; seven minutes past one. He was free all afternoon.

He got up and wandered across to the window, staring out at the playing field, the goal posts, the big tree in the far corner.

All those handsome cowboys!

You're so adventurous!

You'll have to chaperone those girls, Miss Britnell!

A stampede was probably too much to hope for.

The tree stood in the furthest corner of the field, the wire-mesh fence forming a right angle behind its trunk. Behind the fence, the neat divided gardens of duplexes, the back galleries all painted battleship grey. It was a large tree. Not maple. Umbrella-shaped. Probably the only large tree left in the area, the rest sacrificed to the numbered avenues where addresses and directions sounded like Control Tower to navigator. He could look across towards it when he was teaching on the top floor. For weeks now, rooks had been building and squabbling in its topmost branches. He had seen them beating across the field, flopping about ungainly in the tree's crown thrashing the thin branches, heard their cawing as he taught. It irritated him that he didn't know what kind of tree it was.

The bell rang. One-twenty. Teachers began to drift out leaving behind those the Matrics had freed.

Elm? Certainly not oak. And not chestnut.

Could you pass this to Mr. Appleby?

He turned from the window.

Visual Bloody Aid.

Complaints on several occasions, eh, Visual Aid? How would you like to complain about this, V.A.? And this! And my boot in your wizened proverbials.

"Yes, of course," said David sitting down again and adding his signature to the others on the flyleaf of *Canadian Pageant* – part of Follet's retirement gift from the Merrymount Staff.

(Enforced contribution: $3.00)

The major part of the gift was a brass-inlay binnacle and compass inscribed: *To Arthur Ellis Follet from his Merrymount colleagues.*

And may all who sail in her strike a rock.

Lachrymose last rites for Follet – another jollity for Monday's final Staff Meeting.

> *. . . but who will remain with us in spirit . . .*

BARF

One-twenty-five.

Garry stuck his head round the door.

"Hey, Garry!"

"Oh, hi, Dave." He came in, nodding to Bardolini. "I've signed it," he said to Visual Aid.

"I was looking for you," said David. "Where've you been?"

Garry sat down in the armchair vacated by Hubnichuk.

"Been stuck in the office all morning. Seen this?"

He handed across a copy of *Saturday Review.*

"The Ciardi essay'd interest you. Give it back to me, though, when you're finished or stick it in my box, O.K.?"

"Thanks. You don't have any spare cigarettes, do you?"

"Keep them," said Garry. "I've got some more in my desk."

"What are you doing, then?" said David.

"Just ploughing through some guidance files with Brunhoff. Some information I need."

David nodded.

"Thesis?"

Garry shrugged and pulled a face.

"Anyway," he said. "Better get back to it. Don't lose that. Stick it in my box if you don't see me."

David turned to the book reviews but just as he started to read, Sid, the junior jockstrap, backed into the Common Room concluding a loud conversation with a kid in the corridor. David put the magazine aside and watched him.

Cropped hair, singlet blinding, Sid sat down opposite Bardolini. His nipples poked at the cotton as if exercise had strengthened them. He put his feet on the coffee-table; his white gym-shoes dazzled. He always wore grey military-looking trousers, a strip of black braid down each seam. A keen disciplinarian, he smelled students' breath when they came out of the washrooms to see if they'd been smoking. At staff meetings, he denounced laxness. He spoke much of "shaping-up" and "cutting the mustard."

Sid looked across and nodded; David nodded back and returned to the magazine.

Sid then engaged Henry in a loud discussion on mufflers.

Henry urged the virtue of additives.

Sid had starter-motor trouble.

Henry suffered with his wiring.

David got up and went out into the corridor. He wandered along looking at the examples of student art and the House Shields celebrating the victors in basketball, football, baseball, hockey and wrestling, until he came to the rear entrance of the gymnasium. He was nominally a member of Blue House. He went down the steps and out onto the playing field.

It was bright and hot; sunlight glinted off parked cars and flashed on windows. He strolled along the side of the school towards the wire-mesh fence. Sid frightened him. *The face that burned a thousand books.* As a caption for a photograph in a cheap paperback biography. Hairy paper. He reached the fence and walked onto the grass. And for the judge's summation . . . *stupidity allied with enthusiasm.* The field sloped towards the fence, a slope almost imperceptible but the ground at the edge of the field was still soggy from the thaw even after weeks of nearly dry weather.

And profile-journalism . . . *his face conveyed that impression of baffled intelligence often seen in monkeys.* But it wasn't really funny. Sid wasn't a joke. The earth, bare in patches near the fence, held his footprints like plasticene but didn't stick to his shoe. Chandler could have fixed the bugger exactly . . . *eyes like a gull.* That sort of thing. But better.

As he neared the tree, he heard a loud cawing behind him. He smiled as he saw a rook up on the roof of the school perched sentinel on the TV aerial. Strange how big they looked even at a distance. He liked their wariness, their wildness. If they nested near houses, unlike swallows or pigeons, they remained independent. They graced in-

155

habited areas with their presence, their gleaming blackness, but remained aloof, suspicious.

Tough, lordly birds. He liked their cawing; it was at once wild and homely, a sound which always brought a rush of feelings. As a child, he'd always associated them with the Northmen. Thistles, too. It seemed that rooks had always been there in his childhood round farms and houses, their *caw-caw* blending into his dreams as the light of summer evenings filtered through the curtains.

He sat down on a long root raised above the bare earth and leaned against the trunk.

From his uncle's yard, the field sloped down to a hedge, a road, and beyond that the bottom field before the brook. Every detail incised on his memory, the grey and yellow lichened gate-post, chickweed at his feet, purple vetch thick in the hedge-bottom, and in the far field black on orange, three rooks perched on the stooked sheaves.

Like stills from a movie.

Another.

Rooks like an insane painting.

He'd been walking up a steep field. The wind was blowing from behind driving a grey drizzle. The pasture had been sown with a special fodder, long blue-green grass, and a herd of Frisians was huddled in the centre of the field in a rectangle of electric fence. He had reached the top of the field and climbed the stile and fields had sloped away in front of him, the hedges smaller and smaller, towards the village. Behind a clump of distant trees, the grey spire of the village church. The long grass was running like a sea.

Three large trees stood in the corner of the hedge and as he approached rooks had started to fly up, circling, drifting, cawing, thirty of them, forty, until they were boiling out of the tree tops. The sky flung with black wings.

That moment, black birds and grey sky, and he had felt an intruder and gone back to the top of the field, skirting the rookery, trudging on through the rain half a mile out of his way.

The rook on the school roof *caw-cawed* again and then launched into heavy, measured flight towards the row of duplexes. It landed on the edge of a roof nearer him. Two houses further down a woman in curlers came out onto her gallery with a green garbage bag and the rook lifted away.

He looked at his watch and getting up, strolled back towards the school with its rows of glittering windows.

In the Common Room Sid was still talking to Henry. He sat down at the far end of the settee again and picked up the magazine. The shiny pages stuck to his sweaty fingers.

Henry scorned the efficacy of rust-proofing.

Sid thought it the Board's duty to supply outlets for block-heaters.

Henry swore by studded tires.

Sid would like a few more statistics about these foreign cars.

"Way to go, Howie!" shouted Sid. "Way to go!"

David looked up.

"Congratulations!" said Bardolini.

Bunceford was standing in the doorway glowing pink, beaming and nodding.

"Unexpected," he mumbled, "had no idea."

He mopped his brow and pate.

"Ah, come on!" said Sid. "You must of put in for it months ago."

"What's the occasion?" said David.

"Principal of Merrydale Elementary," said Sid. "Negotiating on a separate contract now, eh Howie?"

"Well . . ." said Bunceford, "one applies – in general, you know, and – just luck this time . . ."

"No!" said Bardolini. "No surprise to see your name."

"You deserve every inch of it," said Sid.

David smiled and nodded at Bunceford and, glancing up at the clock above the door, went out into the corridor again. He walked along to the Office and looked on the Principal's Notice Board. He took down the sheaf of mimeographed papers and turned them until he reached Merrymount.

Bunceford.

Transfers	Brunhoff, G.	Snowdon High
	Renfrew, A.	Windsor High

Promotion to Department Head

	Larkshur, R.	Auto/Electric
	Speers, N.	English
	Weinbaum, M.	History
	Westlake, G.	Guidance

David stared at white paper, purple print.

The bell rang.

Jim's *Volkswagen* was parked across the road from the school's side entrance. As David walked down the steps, he took off his jacket and, undoing the top button of his shirt, stripped off his tie. He opened the car door and bundled the jacket and tie into the back seat.

"Well that didn't last long," said Jim.

"What's this?"

"Oh, stick it in the back. It's a *Wexler* test – I'm working tonight."

David got in and slammed the door shut.

"Let's get moving," he said, "get some air. It's hot as hell in here."

"So . . ." said Jim.

"Who's the work for? Research Associates?" said David.

"I phoned the guy this morning again and I've got work every night and every day if I want it. *And* recognition for the M.Ed."

"How come? I thought you said they were backing off before."

"They've just got a government contract testing adults – Manpower or something. Money for old rope, mate. Administering and evaluating *Kuder Preference, Wexler,* and *Minnesota Multiphasal.* More work than they can handle."

Past a *Colonel Sander's* outlet, a revolving tub on a thirty-foot pole.

GIVE HER A NIGHT OFF. TAKE HOME A BUCKET OF CHICKEN.

"So you're in the money," said David.

"Minimum twenty-five bucks an hour," said Jim.

"Jesus . . ."

"I *told* you, old son. I *told* you. A bit of paper from McGill, join a professional association, and you can print the bloody stuff."

Past gaunt concrete boxes of an apartment building under construction.

NOW RENTING

By its side, its finished twin.

NOW OPEN FOR YOUR ADMIRATION

"So," said Jim. "How did it go?"

"O.K."

"Little lecture about hairy goodies, was it?"

"That sort of thing."

Turning west on Sherbrooke.

"Lovely!" said Jim. "That's the sort of stuff I like to hear!"

A row of gingerbread Victorian houses, the boom of a giant crane motionless above them.

"Stern exhortations!" said Jim.

TEPERMAN WRECKING

"Ernest appeals to one's higher nature!"

Torn gaps, now asphalt car-parks.

"Gone, oh gone are the gropes of yesteryear!" cried Jim. "Eschewed is the student body! No more the naughty nookie!"

"That's about it," said David.

"So there you are, you see," said Jim.

He leaned over and switched on COXM.

"Oh!" he said. "I've booked a *U-Haul* for Monday night, O.K.?"

"O.K."

"So you'll have to sign that lease tomorrow or Sunday."

David nodded.

Running down the Scoreboard now . . .

"*Must* we suffer this?" said David.

And the temperature in Our Town – a beautiful 79 COXM *degrees.*

"How can they *listen* to that shit!" said David.

"And you can spend the year looking for another job," said Jim.

"What?"

"Well you're not going to get any promotion under the Board, are you?"

"I suppose not," said David.

Past the hideous *Holiday Inn.*

He wondered what cynicisms were taught at McGill and the University of Montreal under the name of architecture.

"I'm going to drop you at Sherbrooke and Guy," said Jim. "I've got to see someone at four."

"O.K."

"You going to be in at above five?"

"I expect so, yes."

"Something I want to show you," said Jim.

David hopped out at the lights. He thought for a moment of going back along Sherbrooke to look in the window of *The Petit Musée*; he'd glimpsed a Tang horse as they drove past. Mr. Klein would let him handle it, run his fingers over the soft, thick glaze. But he really couldn't be bothered. He was already sweating. He turned west on Lincoln past *La Source*. He was tempted by memory of the cool dim interior – a fast beer to deal with his thirst followed by a slow double whisky. The beer like brass. Or maybe a pernod. He could taste its faint sweetness surrounding its bitter fire. Oily. But he walked on; he didn't want to keep Susan hanging about near the phone she used in the shopping-centre.

When he got home, he took off his shirt and socks and flopped down in his armchair. He didn't feel like reading. After a while, he got up and wandered into the kitchen. He discovered a *Coke* in the fridge but it made him thirstier. He checked his wallet. After Susan called, he'd phone out for beer. He read the labels on some tins and packages in the cupboard.

He looked into Jim's room; his books and clothes already packed up in cardboard boxes, corded.

The tiled floor in the bathroom was cool. He thought of having a bath. But it was too much effort. He put the plug in the washbasin and turned on the cold tap. He put his hands flat in the basin while it filled. He stood staring down at the tiny air bubbles trapped in the hairs on his wrists.

"What do you mean, 'What do I mean'? Because it was like a TV episode, that's why. Every cliché in the book."

"You know. He said everything you'd expect him to say."

David turned the paper round and started placing dots inside the rows of circles.

"No. He didn't really mention you."

"Well, he didn't accuse me of breathing on the crown jewels, as it were."

"No, all he said was 'relationship.' The whole thing was only about ten minutes."

He gave the circles corkscrew tails.

"Yes, just a lot of circumlocution, that's all."

"It means round-about ways of saying things."

"Sorry."

"I've *told* you – I can't remember exactly. Nothing much. He was just being earnest about teachers being like parents and about my future, that kind of thing. General uplifting moral advice – you know what he's like. A sort of Polonius act."

He started to fill in every second circle.

"Nothing much. I was there to be talked *at*. Nodded mostly, I suppose. Did faces."

"Umm?"

"There wasn't much I *could* say."

"Except the little matter of the library books, sweetheart. You're forgetting that, aren't you?"

He started doing chain-mail on the other side of the paper.

"No, I didn't have to say anything. I suppose he assumed it from the fact I was there."

"Yes, I suppose so."

"Oh, for Christ's sake! No, listen! It was *funny*."

"Yes! Funny's exactly the word I'd choose."

"Well, you weren't there, were you?"

He added swords to the stick-figures by lengthening arms and drawing cross-hilts.

"No. Of course I didn't mean that. But really, Susan. It *was*. It really was. Like a scene from a *Carry On* film or *Lucky Jim* or something."

"Well you know what he's like – pompous dwarf."

"O.K."

"No. I really didn't."

The pencil scribbling round and round – a bird's nest of lines.

"O.K. Suppose I had. And where would *that* have got us. Or more to the point, where would it have got *me*!"

"Charming."

"Thank you, thank you. Very nice."

"Jesus Christ! *Clean!* This is me, Dave Appleby, Susan. We're in Montreal, right? I'm not the mother in fucking *Ben Hur*, you know!"

"What?"

"Just like that, eh? For Christ's sake, Susan! Don't be so fucking *childish*!"

BRRR.   BRRR.   BRRR.

David went down the passage and let Jim in.

"Get your things on," said Jim.

"I'm on the phone."

"Wait till you see what your Uncle Jim's got outside."

David went back and picked up the receiver.

"Look!" he said.

The dial tone hummed in his ear.

He looked at the vast white car. Whitewall tires. Glittering hub-caps. Red upholstery with sparkly lines in it. A shiny radio aerial.

"As big as the bloody *Queen Elizabeth*, isn't it?"

"What's the point of being in North America," said Jim, "unless one enjoys vulgar gestures?"

David patted the top of the car; it was hot.

"Trunk," said Jim, opening it up.

David looked at the spare tire inside.

"Very roomy," he said.

They sat in the front with the doors open. Jim pulled levers and pressed switches, turned the radio on and off.

"Plenty of leg-room," said David.

"Power-steering," said Jim. "Drive with one finger."

"How are you going to pay for it?"

"Well I'd ordered it even before there was a chance of this testing – but *now*."

Poop!

He sounded the horn.

"No problem."

He adjusted the seat again.

"What one needs," he said, "is *style*. That's the thing. None of this threadbare graduate-student stuff. Know why?"

Gagnon was slumped on a wooden kitchen chair in a patch of shade near the front door of the building.

"Because over here, you get largely what you assume you're going to get. And people give you what they assume you're worth. And on what, pray, do they base their assumptions?"

He patted the wheel.

Black trousers, a stained T-shirt, and red knitted carpet slippers. The neck and shoulders of a quart bottle of *Molson* rose from his fat thighs.

"Not bad, eh?" said Jim. "*Galaxy 500*."

"It's very nice, Jim. Very comfortable."

The defective boy from the Polish grocery wove into view riding against the traffic. He swerved towards the curb in front of the car, and standing on the pedals, bucked the bike up onto the pavement. He shot towards the front door of the building, leaping off backwards just before the bike struck.

"Is that for me?" called David. "Apartment 307?"

"See you later, then," said Jim. "I'm going to check these tire pressures and then I'm going straight on to work."

"Posh, Jim," said David as he slammed the door.

Jim pulled away from the curb and waved.

As David was paying the delivery boy, Gagnon said, "Hey!"

David pretended not to hear.

"Hey. That your car?"

He looked down at Gagnon's grey brush-cut, at the great slope of paunch, the distended trouser-legs.

"Partly," he said. "Half of it."

"New, eh?" said Gagnon.

David nodded.

"Hot like hell, eh?" said Gagnon.

"Yes," said David, nodding.

"My car's a *Buick*," said Gagnon. "Give me the money and I buy a *Buick*."

"Well," said David, shrugging, "we're well pleased with that one."

"Sure thing!" said Gagnon. "With a *Ford* you got yourself a good car."

David hoisted the case of beer.

"How long those guys going to stay out?" said Gagnon, jerking his head at the case. "The liquor there. Five weeks now, eh?"

"About that," said David.

"*Me*, I don't care," said Gagnon. "I got all the liquor I can drink. But five weeks, that's not funny."

"Especially on days like this," smiled David.

"The government should stop that," said Gagnon. "Five weeks – *sacrament!* Five weeks is five weeks."

"Those guys were working for fifty bucks," said David.

"Sure," said Gagnon. "If guys don't want to work – *pataud!*"

"Well . . ."

"Yes, sir! With a new *Ford* you got no problems."

"Anyway," said David, hitching the case higher under his arm, "we can still get beer."

"Me, I got all the liquor in the world. You don't believe me? *In the world.*"

164

"Very nice," said David.

"Go on, my frien' – you say a kind that you like."

David shrugged.

"Oh, I don't know. I like most of them."

"The name of one that you like."

"Oh, pernod, I suppose."

"You want to take a pernod?" demanded Gagnon, heaving himself up from the chair.

"Well, that's very nice of you, but I . . ."

"I think you don't want to drink with me."

"No, no. Of course not," said David. "It's just . . ."

"Sure," said Gagnon. "We'll take a pernod. Pernod, rye, whisky, gin – *krisse,* no problem! Gin, rum, sherry, that white one there . . ."

"Well, I really mustn't be long . . ." said David as he followed Gagnon's waddling bulk into the dim foyer.

"This weather – *sacrament!*" said Gagnon, as he unlocked the apartment door – "it makes you thirsty like a prick."

The smell.

The smell was rank and nearly made him gag. He tried shallow breathing. Shit certainly, piss, cooking, old sweat – but the sum was greater than the parts. Gagnon went into the kitchen alcove to get glasses and David put the case of beer on a kitchen table which stood in the middle of the living room. The table-top was encrusted. Four chrome and plastic chairs. An open package of *Wonder* bread, a melted paper of butter, a bottle of *FBI Cream Soda,* a gallon tin of strawberry jam.

A pair of rubber pants hung from the TV aerial.

A once-pink armchair.

A gutted settee which sprouted yellowing tufts of kapok.

The liquor cabinet was large and baroque: glass doors with diamond-leaded panes and gold hinges, curved legs writhing with gilded scrollwork, cupid door-knobs.

He took the glass of pernod and sat down in the armchair wondering what had trapped him into being there and suffering this Gagnon who was accountable for unforgivable past abuse and hostility. Guilt that Gagnon was French Canadian? Class guilt? Defencelessness in the face of hectoring manners? As the glass touched his lips, he tried not to imagine the kitchen, tried not to think of the unspeakable French-Canadian diseases which were obviously endemic in such an apartment. Such as hookworm, ringworm, venereal disorders, tapeworm, cankers, botulism.

"Eh?" said Gagnon. "That's the *real* good thing."

The drink tasted like aniseed-flavoured maple syrup.

Staring at the plastic potty which sat on the carpet just in front of the chair, he made a judicious face. The potty was half full of piss; a pencil floated in it.

"It's slightly *sweeter* than the kind I've had before. But very good," he added.

Gagnon drained his glass. He sat on the settee with his legs apart to allow his belly to hang down.

"We'll try the whisky," he said.

"Well, I really ought . . ."

"I think you didn't like the pernod."

"No! It was excellent. Excellent," said David.

"The whisky's always good," said Gagnon.

"How about a beer while they're still cold," said David.

"You save your beer," said Gagnon.

On the wall above the settee was a large reproduction of *The Last Supper*; patches of it seemed almost iridescent in the sunlight.

Gagnon poured whisky from a *Haig* bottle into both glasses and brought them over. The whisky tasted only slightly less sweet than the pernod.

"It's got an *unusual* flavour," said David hesitantly. "Very interesting."

"You notice that, eh?"

"Mmmm."

"How much you pay for whisky in the commission there?"

"Oh, eight or nine dollars."

Gagnon held up his glass.

"Seventy-three cents," he said, "*for the gallon.*"

"What do you mean?"

"Steinberg's."

"They don't sell liquor."

"For the whisky taste. How do you say that? The – what you put in."

"In?"

"In the alcool. The *taste,* there."

"Oh, l'essence – the flavour."

"Sure."

"And you put that into alcohol?"

"That's it – but that from the commission, that shit it's not strong like *this.* I have this friend who use to work with me – a big man in *RCA-Victor* there," gesturing towards the window. "A chimiste?"

David nodded.

"He brings me for nothing. *One hundred* per cent."

Gagnon started to roll another cigarette.

God, that it might be pure! Any "big man" in *RCA-Victor* Gagnon was likely to know probably rendered down old records in his basement to extract the alcohol, bubbling the crude through *Mr. Clean* and filtering through an undershirt. Patches of *The Last Supper* were iridescent; glittering; moving. He'd rather be paralysed than blind.

"Your friend there – I think he isn't from Canada."

"He's English," said David, not letting the whisky past his teeth.

"Yes, but I think he isn't from Canada."

"English from England," said David. "Me too."

"You know what we call you guys?" said Gagnon. "Guys from England? Limeys. You ever hear that?"

David smiled and nodded.

"I wonder," he said, "if I could have some water in this? I don't usually . . ."

"That's the real strong stuff," said Gagnon.

"A bit too strong for me without water," said David, shaking his head.

"There's a lot of fog there," said Gagnon.

"Pardon?"

"In England," called Gagnon from the kitchen. "What you call *fog* all the time."

"That's right," said David, taking the jug and thinning the whisky with as much water as he could get into the glass.

They sipped and drank in silence.

He could feel the drink hitting his empty stomach.

Gagnon sighed from time to time; from time to time, apropos of nothing, said *tabernac!* – an expression he seemed to favour.

David was offended by the *naughtiness* of French-Canadian swearing. So *soppy*. Rather like English children saying "Bum." How could one take seriously those who expressed anger, wonder, or disgust by saying, "Oh, Host!", "Receptacle for the Eucharist!" or "Little Box!"

Swimming about somewhere – if "tabernac" did mean the container of the Host rather than "tent" or "church" – the word was, was – *ciborium!*

Definitely something odd about *The Last Supper*. Optic nerves seared by 33⅓ juice.

Records were my downfall, doctor.

Gagnon was so fat that there was no loose in his trouser-legs. His arms were thick and muscled but the skin was pallid. It was the paunch, however, which fascinated David. He observed it covertly. He found himself thinking of "the paunch" and "it" rather than of "Gagnon's paunch" for it seemed somehow independent of Gagnon, an excrescence. It crouched on Gagnon's thighs like a plump animal; like a porridge-filled balloon. Except that "balloon" was misleading as to size. And "garbage bag" was possibly exaggerating.

When he stood, the paunch hung like a little barrel. A little firkin. But the key question – was it hard or soft?

Down, Firkin! Good boy!

In French, garbage bags were called "sacs à ordures." A delightful word, ordure.

What, he wondered, did Firkin look like *naked*? Or, to be more specific, and specificality. Specificity. Try that again. Or, to be more specific, and specificity was always a virtue, how was it *attached*? Was it firm beneath the skin or did it hang like a vast boob?

And dependent on that, if "dependent" was indeed the word he sought, was the whole problem of how Gagnon achieved sexual intercourse. No erection would extend beyond, *could* extend beyond that overhang. *Unless* he was abnormally and mightily endowed or afflicted with giantism of the member – but such endowment or affliction could be discounted because *there was nowhere in his trousers for it to go*. David felt pleased with the logic of this. It would seem, therefore, that the answer was *positional*. Perhaps, lying down, the flesh subsided like a breast and his wife bestrode him?

Were that *not* the case, the words "sexual intercourse" were inadequate. He needed a cumbersome word, dignified, elephantine, a ponderous, lumbering word to do justice to such coupling.

Union?

CONGRESS

"It goes good, the rum there with the coke, eh?" said Gagnon.

"Splendid!" said David.

"Yes, sir!" said Gagnon. "That's a beautiful car. It makes *sense*."

Upstairs in his drawer was a packet of *Ramses* he'd bought yesterday against Susan's coming, if indeed "against" and "coming" were the words he sought . . .

Stop! Stop.

"You want to buy a TV?" said Gagnon.

Susan!

"A colour portable?" said Gagnon.

"I don't usually watch it," said David.

"Twenty-four dollar."

"That seems cheap."

"They cost in the store five hundred, five-fifty. *In the store*," said Gagnon with heavy significance.

"You mean . . .?"

"I got guys I know – any little thing you want, you tell me and I order it for you, O.K.?"

"How much are electric typewriters?"

Gagnon breathed in heavily, shaking his head.

"Now is not the season for typewriters," he said.

David nodded.

"I can get a electric piano," offered Gagnon. "But that's not the same thing."

They sat for some time in an easy silence.

The sherry tasted like cough medicine.

"My frien'," sighed Gagnon. "We're all a bunch of poor pricks."

David nodded.

A key turned in the lock and Mrs. Gagnon came in. She was carrying a sleeping baby and trailed by one of the snotties.

David forced himself up and out of the armchair.

"This is Madame," said Gagnon.

She nodded and said something in rapid French.

David smiled.

"She don't speak English good," said Gagnon.

Madame was wearing shorts and a halter. Green veins snaked and lumped in her white legs. She disappeared with the baby. The kid stood with his back against the wall near the door, staring. He looked as dull as his mother. David turned his foot on some clothes-pegs which were scattered near the chair and sat down again. He pulled out some of the garments which were wadded uncomfortably behind him and dropped them over the arm onto the floor.

"No," he said, "I'll stick with the rum, if you don't mind. I think I liked it better than the sherry and that other one."

He glanced at the child, then stared. The kid's face was bright red, tears starting in his bulging eyes. As David looked, the flush faded, the eyes returned to normal. He wondered if he should mention it. Embarrassing if the child was subject to fits. Normal enough looking now. *Petit mal,* was it called?

It seemed likely.

Madame came through the room and went into the kitchen alcove.

"She only got a few words in English," said Gagnon.

"No, no," said David, "I should be able to speak French."

"You know what she is?" said Gagnon.

He opened his mouth and leaned forward on the couch. His mouth was a black O. He put a fat forefinger into his mouth and waggled it while letting out a falsetto scream.

David stared at him.

"Her," said Gagnon, "she's Indian."

"I've never met an Indian before."

"That's what *she* is," nodded Gagnon.

Was it polite to mention *tribe*? A tricky point of etiquette. Perhaps like asking an Australian what his ancestors had been sent down for? Stick to faces. If indeed, upon mature reflection, Australians, who consumed steaks with eggs on top for breakfast, *would* be? The point *was*, if it *would* bother them.

The kid had come nearer.

"Hello," said David.

Nothing.

"Allo," he essayed.

"He's Réal, that one," said Gagnon.

The kid, still staring and silent, edged nearer. He seemed to be the centre of a strong odour. *Petit mal*, indeed! The centre of a strong ordure. Réal had shat himself, and evilly.

Madame came in and cleared the table; didn't clean it though. Need a hammer and cold chisel for that. Dish and kitchen noises. The coke cut the sweetness of the rum. How could they *sit down* with a load like that in their trousers! To be able to speak real French, French enough to be able to politely hint that something be *done*.

The derrière of Réal is plastered with merde.

Had a fine lilt to it.

Madame talking from the kitchen; Gagnon answering.

Gagnon reclining on the settee; it did subside but did it subside *enough*?

The glass furred with condensation.

"She says do you like pizza and macaroni?"

"Oh, really," said David, "I really don't want to impose, really."

"She made for you, my limey frien'," said Gagnon.

"That's most kind of you. I hadn't realized it was so late. Really very nice of you. I will postpone, I will *abandon* my engagement."

He had wronged this Gagnon.

Tears welled into his eyes as he clasped the honest fellow's work-scarred hand . . .

Something he had said there. Disturbing. He had said . . .?

"I see you looking at my picture there," said Gagnon.

"Sorts of glitter," said David.

"That's a heirloom picture," said Gagnon.

About dinner, it was. He had said . . . . .

"You think," said Gagnon, "she's painted, that picture."

"Can I use the phone?"

"Sure."

Phone-book almost impossible to read. Stupid small print. Wavery. Tracing along the line.

"On that painting," said Gagnon, "I'm telling you is not one, single piece of paint."

As he dialed, he saw letters in the blue carpet.

Woven in red.

TEL.

He stooped on the last digit following the TEL further under the table.

WINDSOR HOTEL

Susan!

I'd have hung up.

I've got to see you.

I love you.

ALL THAT MATTERS IS I LOVE YOU.

And do you?

Susan?

He put the phone down.

"You never guess what she's done with," said Gagnon, "in a *thousand year!*"

"Who's done with?"

"She's done with *wing*!"

He waggled his fingers.

"Papillons wing. *Papillons?*"

"Butterflies," nodded David.

"Tabernac! Butterflies! You ever hear of that thing?"

He bolted the bathroom door. Definitely a little squiffy. Food would fix that. He sat on the edge of the tub. The air was festooned with clothes; he pushed away a pair of nylons that touched his face. The light was fading. Like being a fish in the bottom of an aquarium with the water above crowded with the bright hanging shapes of other fish. Cooler here and lino not those little black and white tiles. Lino with roses. Through the open window, jackfrost glass, he could hear vague traffic noises. He found he was breathing heavily; it was his nose making the whistley noise. He sat on the edge of the tub.

It is a hot summer evening, he thought, *the light is fading, and I am in Montreal, Canada, and I am sitting alone, all alone, in the bathroom of André Gagnon, janitor, feeling sad.*

On a shelf above the end of the bath stood a cut-glass bottle, a length of rubber tubing coming out of it and ending in a net-covered bulb. Scent? Or some strange feminine sexual accessory?

His words. And her words. The precise words spoken.

She had said:

"It matters if *I* love *you.*"

He had said:

"And do you?"

And she had said:

"I don't know . . ."

The lavatory, the lavatory was full of what he hoped were coffee-grounds. He missed the bowl at first burst and steadied himself against the wall with his right hand, leaning forward. He aimed into the slop studying the effect, careful. The porcelain

I don't know . . . she had said . . . *I don't know . . .*

peppered with black specks.

He pushed himself upright and worked the flush. Tumbled nature's germens. A golden bottle of shampoo on the window-sill. He peered at the fine print.

173

Versez un peu de shampooing dans la paume de votre main et appliquez aux cheveux.

Bent closer; definitely "shampooing." Something wrong about that; wrong part of speech or something. An odd people, the French. Merely another instance.

He looked at himself in the dim mirror.

Undersea.

A Welsh accent sounding in his head.

If that wasn't coffee-grounds, boyo, someone in this house was in a bad way!

"Why," he said aloud to his reflection, "are the British so amused by lavatory humour?"

Tears were running down his cheeks.

The light in the room was failing fast; Gagnon, save for the white glimmer of his T-shirt, was becoming an indistinct mound on the couch. The window was pearly.

David lay back in the armchair, Réal heavy on his chest and stomach, listening to Gagnon's deepening snores and staring at a glint of light on the edge of the TV set.

He felt less well.

The pizza had been the frozen kind without much cheese and withered. The macaroni had been naked.

Madame seemed to have disappeared again.

"We're all alone, Réal," he whispered.

He felt the tiny tremors of Réal's fingers on his chest, warm. *The Last Supper* was a dark shape on the wall, the frame a darker rectangle. The furniture shapes were coming in and out of focus. He held the glass at his lip breathing into it, the dregs lukewarm and flat.

He would phone again.

"Where's your mummy, Réal?" he whispered.

He looked down at the little coconut head.

Mr. Woods, his name. With big coloured pictures and a pointer.

Up and down the rows. "La table," Monsieur Woods. "La fenêtre," Monsieur Woods. "Des livres," Monsieur.

"Ou est votre maman, Réal?"

The child clutched.

"You don't want to go, do you, little nubbins? Little shitty drawers. Little pong-poo. Shall I tell you a story? Would you like that?"

Whispering, David began the story of Goldilocks. After he had done the three bear voices the first time, he stopped.

"You don't understand a word of this," he said.

His head was throbbing with the effort of talking. The falsetto squeak of Baby Bear had brought him close to retching. But he felt it somehow important to finish the story for the kid. Against Gagnon's snores, he whispered on.

". . . and Goldilocks had been *so* frightened that she never, *never*, went there again."

She never went there again, repeated the voice inside his head. *She never went there again.*

He forced himself up in the chair and looked at the sleeping child's face. He worked himself to the edge of the chair and, Réal in his arms, got to his feet. The room reeled. He placed the child back in the armchair and, banging his thigh against the table, made his way round it to the door.

He smashed into the newel-post at the foot of the stairs and nearly fell. It hurt his shoulder and chest. A sliding sea of black and white tiles.

She never went there again, said the voice.

I think I'll phone.

"Stop saying things."

I think, said the voice, *I'll phone.*

His mouth was filling with clear, salty saliva; he knew he was going to be sick. He stumbled against someone's door on a landing. He fell on the third flight of stairs, raking his head on the bannisters.

It hit me when I got up, said the voice, repeating, repeating.

She had said.

He had said.

And she had said.

And she had said.

He got the door open and lurched along the wall fumbling for the bathroom light. Kneeling over the lavatory, he waited, dribbling and spitting out saliva as it flooded into his mouth. The lavatory bowl smelled, amplified the sounds of his breathing. His shirt was plastered to his back; he could feel sweat running from his arm-pits; cold sweat starting out on his face. He was shivering. Sparkling dots of light buzzing in the darkness like a snowstorm of interference on a TV. He was only half conscious, swaying. The buzzing dark shifting. His stomach heaved, snatching him forward. A small mouthful of bile and slop splashed into the toilet bowl.

Help me, Jim! cried the voice.

CRAMP!

He shot out his left leg and fell against the wall. His body writhed. The muscles in his neck started to knot and jump. He clutched at the hard lumps, jerked his head in agony. His stomach contracted again and again but nothing came out.

Jim! Jim! I'm dying!

The darkness fading, the screen of prickling light thinned and slowly cleared.

Knotted muscles still jumped in his legs.

He found himself lying on the floor, his head beside the base of the toilet bowl. The unshaded light bulb was burning into his eyes. He looked away and glowing bulbs swam down the walls. He turned his face against the coolness of the white stand, stretching his left leg, straining it straight.

Not drunk. Not drunk. This wasn't drunk.

Some of the vomit had come down his nose. He snuffled and slimy lumps came into his mouth, his throat. He worked them forward to his lips and tried to spit them out.

The loud breathing was his own.

He struggled up onto his knees. He had smashed in the side of the wicker clothes basket. The water in the bowl was cloudy; the side of the bowl splattered. Where water trickled in at the back of the bowl, a tiny current agitated particles of vomit. Sinking, wavering to the surface again.

A coiled pubic hair on the white rim.

A bottle of *Mr. Clean* on the floor behind the lavatory.

His temples were wet; his hands glistening with sweat.

He leaned further over and opened his mouth wide. His stomach fought. Saliva. Muscles in his forearm cramping, solid with pain.

Pushing up on the lavatory, hauling on the towel-rail, trembling, he got himself on his feet. He staggered along the passage towards his bedroom, his legs, weakened by cramps, giving way under him. He fell onto his bed. He closed his eyes. The gloom started to shift and lurch. He opened his eyes and put one foot on the floor.

His stomach heaved and he gushed vomit. He had only time to turn his head on the pillow. And again. He forced himself up, vomiting over the sheet, across the sill, and rauking into the night. Again and again like a snow-blower gorging an attendant truck. He could hear the spatter of it falling.

Four feet away a window squawked up.

He could not lift his head.

"You dairty bastard!" said the Scots lady. "You're disgusting! Could you no go to the bathroom!"

The window slammed shut.

"I've been poisoned," he whispered.

Dribble hanging cold on his chin.

His throat scraped raw.

Cold. Shivering cold.

"Poisoned."